THE MEETING PLACE

THE MEETING PLACE

Mary Hocking

Chatto & Windus

LONDON

First published in the UK in 1996

1 3 5 7 9 10 8 6 4 2
Copyright © Mary Hocking 1996

Mary Hocking has asserted her right under the Copyright, Designs
and Patents Act 1988 to be identified as the author of this work.

First published in the United Kingdom in 1996 by
Chatto & Windus Limited
Random House, 20 Vauxhall Bridge Road
London SW1V 2SA

Random House Australia (Pty) Limited
20 Alfred Street, Milsons Point, Sydney
New South Wales 2061, Australia

Random House New Zealand Limited
18 Poland Road, Glenfield
Auckland 10, New Zealand

Random House South Africa (Pty) Limited
PO Box 337, Bergvlei 2012, South Africa

Random House UK Limited Reg. No. 954009

A CIP catalogue record for this book
is available from the British Library

ISBN 0 7011 6528 6

Typeset in Bembo by SX Composing, Rayleigh, Essex
Printed and bound in Great Britain by
Mackays of Chatham, PLC, Chatham, Kent

One

ON THE way, Clarice turned into a lane with a signpost pointing in the direction of an old town on a hill that looked inviting across the intervening fields. She needed something inviting.

Clarice Mitchell would have chosen to describe herself, if pressed to do so tiresome a thing, as a capable, no-nonsense person, not by choice but through the circumstances of life. Perhaps by choice she would have been passionate, wild, given to great loves, her life an unco-ordinated series of amorous adventures. Perhaps. But the face that had looked back at her in the mirror each morning for sixty-nine years told her she wasn't modelled that way – had told her so this morning in no uncertain terms. She was small. Everything about her was small, hands, feet, thighs, breasts, all nicely proportioned but small; the Cleopatras were outside her range, the only Shakespearean role she had ever been offered was Mustard Seed. And that was a bit of Freudian casting, for there was more than a suggestion of mustard in her constitution. The eyes, widely spaced, were considerate; the eyes of an observer rather than a dreamer. The puckered mouth suggested that what was observed would be shrewdly evaluated. Ever since she could remember she had been plagued by a prickly intelligence. She hadn't asked for it, it was just there, like red hair or a Roman nose; there was nothing one could do about it, so one must learn to live with it. That, she supposed, might well have been her predominant attitude to life, accepting what was given and getting on with it, without making a fuss. She hated fuss. So why was she fussing now, driving so slowly up this innocent country lane as if she were heading for the city of dreadful night instead of a one-time county town long relegated to historic village status? And why had she taken this detour, anyway?

Perhaps the problem lay in accepting the given of this particular occasion. She was making the detour because she needed to pause, and so she had turned off the A road and headed for the old town. It had looked inviting in its retirement, standing back from the modern world that had rejected it, a little lordly on its slight incline. But it was not as near as it had seemed. On either side were green fields and knots of trees behind which old red-brick houses took refuge – a picture conveying that overall sense of placid calm that the English countryside so well contrives. Clarice noted swallows lined up on telephone wires ready for departure and further on a magpie flew from a thicket. She muttered, 'One for sorrow,' and couldn't recall what one was supposed to say to appease the fates if its partner failed to put in an appearance. The hedges were high and she could not see the town as she approached; even after a reassuring sign that proclaimed she had arrived, it seemed to want to hide itself.

When eventually she had parked in what she took to be the main street, broad and tree-lined, the pale stone buildings sensible straight up and down, she sat for a few minutes letting her eye take in the scene, appreciating the contrasts of light and shade.

High time she was behaving like this old town, with its cool, silvery look, she told herself; put some distance between herself and the modern world with all its stresses and strains. She got out of the car and turned towards the street, pleasantly full of purpose, but by the time she was sitting at the window of a quiet lounge bar, supplied with soup and a glass of wine, she was aware of her own particular stresses and strains. She was conscious of her breathing; not breathless, but conscious of the mechanism. Her body was like her car, it laboured and needed frequent servicing. Grudgingly she allowed it a pill.

The eating area — it was scarcely a restaurant — affected the appearance of a private house; it was almost empty, as were the streets of the town. 'Our season is really over now,' the proprietor said when she remarked on this. He sounded mildly defensive but was mollified by her enquiry about the stone. 'Blue lias and sandstone.' They agreed that the effect was very pleasing. Four women came and sat at a table near the bar and he went to serve them. Clarice found herself drumming her fingers. The soup was both wholesome and appetising; it was also very hot. She tended to rush her meals, but, as this would not be possible, it seemed a good opportunity to study the notes handed out to members of the company by the Theatre Club director. Last chance to turn back, she thought wryly as she sipped the wine. It was only half a joke.

When the invitation had come from the Beacon Theatre Company she had not at first intended to volunteer her services. She valued the involvement with the local amateur theatre. Her own work as a painter tended to be solitary and she did not enjoy socialising for its own sake, so the opportunity to join with others engaged, however modestly, even at times ineptly, in creative endeavour was important to her. But the idea of putting on a performance in another company's theatre did not appeal to her. The Beacon was well known in the world of amateur theatre, and not only for its unusual location; its standards were formidably high and its facilities for rehearsal were the envy of many larger companies. The opportunity, not only to mount a production there but to rehearse in one of the old barns, was not to be missed, the director had informed her. Clarice had been about to say that this was one opportunity she was prepared to miss when it suddenly came to her that the name of the place was familiar for reasons quite unconnected with theatre.

'I once knew someone whose grandmother was born in that farm,' she had exclaimed, reading the letter from the Beacon Theatre Company.

That someone had been Clarice's headmistress and until this moment Clarice had never given a thought to the occasionally mentioned grandmother, let alone the remote farm where she had been born. Miss Wilcox had sprung fully formed into Clarice's life; the fact that she had begetters had seemed irrelevant, if not actually implausible. Hers was the reality of the immortals of fiction. Now, re-reading the letter, Clarice saw and heard Miss Wilcox with the vividness of actuality rather than memory. She was saying:

'We are unique, each one of us, and our life is our unique gift. But it needs to be released, because it has been locked up by the forces of custom and convention. I intend to release your life.' As she spoke she raised her arms. She was a woman of generous proportions, physical and emotional, and the sleeves of her gown seemed to envelop the children so that they saw themselves in a dark cavern and believed that Miss Wilcox would indeed free them from it. Miss Wilcox, hovering above them like a vast, benign bat, had one last word. 'And when I have released you, you must still beware of expectation – your own as well as that of others.'

When she first read the letter from the Beacon Theatre Company, Clarice had felt she had received an imperative to go to the source of Miss Wilcox's magic. Now, sitting in this small lounge, waiting for the soup to cool, she felt a belated need to rationalise the impulse. Much of her life had been spent torn between her father's rationality and Miss Wilcox's irrationality.

'A good time to be travelling,' the proprietor said, pausing by her table. 'Fewer cars on the road.'

'But not sensible.'

A little perplexed, he moved on.

Clarice folded the letter and put it back in her bag. Despite her misgivings, she knew she did not intend to turn back. But it hadn't been a sensible decision. There was no denying that lately, very gradually, the capable, no-nonsense Clarice Mitchell had started to part company with another, more unpredictable person who lived in deep seclusion, making only rare, but uncomfortably telling, forays into the outer world. One such appearance had put an end to what had promised to be a distinguished career in education. Order had been restored since then, but only because Clarice had agreed to change her way of life to accommodate the recluse. If it came to a parting, Clarice knew with whom she would be left. She had no wish for the recluse to take charge of this present enterprise and it was in order to call the no-nonsense person into service that she had stopped here, in this quiet old town so harmoniously set among the small green fields and gently sloping hills.

For a time, she thought the strategy had worked. After leaving the eating place, she found the Quaker meeting house further down the road and sat for a time enjoying the familiar peace. When she left the town she was admirably relaxed at the wheel and philosophical about the farm vehicles, so like prehistoric creatures that have slipped their notch in time. She amused herself by visualising a series of illustrations which might accompany a fable on these lines.

Three-quarters of an hour later, driving through open country, she was aware of the ground rising almost imperceptibly mile by mile, and realised she was nearing her destination.

Nearing, or leaving behind? She asked herself this question when she stopped at a viewing point. She got out of the car and walked to the low stone wall that edged the parking bay. Leaving behind seemed to be the answer, for what now lay beneath her was the country through which she had passed. She seemed, standing here, to belong more to air than earth. She looked towards earth with detached interest.

Immediately in front of her, blown grass on the hillside and the moving shadows of cloud. Far below, land laid out in patterns of activity; marshy levels that were ancient, the lay-out of fields that was medieval, intersected by roads and scattered with buildings that modern needs had imposed on them. She saw the relationship between roads and bridges, farm and hamlet, river and estuary; she observed how tracks, thin as veins, allowed passage through the marshes, and her eyes followed the line of a disused railway that had been superseded by a motorway serving the industrial needs of the distant city to the north. She saw the remains of an old fort sticking out of a field like a broken tooth, the restored water-mill that she had inspected only yesterday, and far on the horizon the chimneys of a power station.

This is history, she thought, delighted. I hope they bring children up here to demonstrate: history, so often taught as a linear development, here seen as a tapestry, past and present co-existent. She looked at it, stretched out beneath, the nature of the land and the patterns of life it nourished, the events it recorded – the detritus of battles fought between armies long since departed and the continuing battle with the hungry sea, presently quiescent beyond the no-man's-land of the marshes. In this setting of sowing and reaping, commerce and industry, the achievements and the mistakes were indelibly imprinted on the land, not to be smoothed away but incorporated, lived with and borne into the future that perhaps was also laid out before her, although she had not the eyes to see it.

There was an edge to the wind she hadn't noticed before. A billowing canopy of cloud had appeared, from the outer edges of which cones and tufts and wedges emerged as if someone had torn frantically at a great bale of cotton-wool. She turned back to the car park and saw, high above a scrubby hill, a tangle of brown fern and discouraged heather across which was scrawled the illusion of a path that seemed to hang on with difficulty and might at some stage lose its hold and slither down into that other world below.

She had only one reminder of that other world once she had left the car park. Bracken and stunted trees obscured the view but at one point, at a turn of the path, there was a gate hung with an old tyre and tangled wire, and through this gap was a distant view of patchworked fields, limelit in a shaft of sunlight. Thereafter the track commanded her full attention. It climbed and climbed and eventually levelled out, rewarding her with nothing. Nothing, that is to say, but gorse and heather running dun into the distance. Nothing here to distract the attention, clutter the mind, charm the eye. On the gritty road ahead water gleamed inkily. Once here, the stages of her journey fell away, clean out of her mind. No other world seemed possible, though world was hardly the right word to describe something that seemed to have existed before worlds had been thought out properly. She was tired now and couldn't handle her ideas. She let it be, and after this it was as if she had consented to something, although she didn't know what, and was only aware of some change in her thinking or perhaps that she had now left thinking behind. Once, when the track narrowed, she said aloud, 'If I go on I may not be able to turn back . . . ' She went on and forgot about it.

The track should by now have joined what passed for a main road across the moorland. 'What do you mean by main road?' a friend had asked dubiously when Clarice had shown her the route she intended to take. 'I mean one that goes from here to there without endlessly wiggling about and has been allotted a colour – in this case, yellow.' There was no sign of the yellow road and the track was descending, which Clarice was sure it shouldn't have done; worse still, it wiggled incessantly. Banks rose steeply on either side and trees arched ahead. She stopped and opened the window. There was the sound of water running.

She needed to ask the way. But how, when she was on her own in what was apparently uninhabited land? It was then, at a sharp bend where she couldn't possibly stop, that she saw the woman. It was as if some unseen hand had thrown an old painting down in front of her; a woman standing in a rocky pool formed by a spring. On the verge there was a long pole with bundles tied to it. The mouth of the stream was hidden in vegetation, but Clarice could see water cascading down the side of the bank. The noise must have blocked out the sound of the car, for the woman did not turn her head and all Clarice glimpsed of her was a tangle of unkempt tawny hair. Her dress was wrapped up around her thighs. Scarcely a walker's outfit, so with any luck, unbelievable though it might seem, she was a native and could give directions, if not to the Beacon Theatre, then to the yellow road. She might even be grateful for a lift. Clarice stopped the car on the far side of the bend. It completely blocked the track, but as she had come to think of it as her private road, this did not concern her. She scrambled out and went back to the spring. The woman had gone. Clarice said loudly, 'I don't believe this!' She was contemplating clambering up the bank when there was the sound of footsteps and a man appeared, a man in corduroys and muddy wellington boots who had every appearance of knowing where he was. He accepted her statement that she was lost without surprise and, despite never having heard of the Beacon Theatre, confidently identified her route for her when shown the sketch map with which she had been provided. As she drove away, Clarice felt a tinge of regret that she and the woman had not even exchanged the wayfarers' smile as their paths crossed.

The farmer's directions were clear, which was fortunate because the only human beings Clarice saw as she drove along the yellow road were two people on horseback and they were some distance away. Above her, dark purple cloud; on either side, long bands of hills, one behind the other, a dull burnish on them in the foreground, in the distance a thumb smear of charcoal on the skyline. She was relieved when she reached the farm.

It had once been a wayside inn, so she had heard. That would have been a long time ago, but when she had her first sight of it, this was how it seemed: a staging post. She stopped some distance from the building. When she switched off the engine and opened the window she could hear water running and recalled that ever since she climbed on to the moor there had been the sound of hidden running water and the soughing of wind.

She felt unjustifiably tired by her journey and something more than that, a tense exhaustion as though she had pushed herself to some limit. She did not want immediately to leave the shelter of the car. She sat back and felt the wind cold against her cheek while she studied the house, as if she had the option of deciding this wasn't what she wanted and could push on somewhere else.

It had been built above a steep-sided valley; being close to where a spring of water rises, the site must always have had an attraction for settlers. Although it stood on high ground, surprising in this area where most dwellings were in the valley, the land to the south swept upward, fold on fold, giving some shelter. The oldest, two-storey part of the house, was built in the middle of the sixteenth century and low, one-storey extensions had been added later on either side. The result was a long, narrow house, well bedded in its green surround. The stonework, light with a hint of blue, was attractive and might have graced a more impressive structure – and in fact had, for the farmhouse, built at the time of the dissolution of the monasteries, was on the site of a small priory.

This was an area that had largely escaped recorded history and little was known about the priory, or the manor that replaced it. It was not Clarice's idea of a manor, but no doubt life in this wild place had been fairly basic in the sixteenth century and the dwelling, which she saw as being just about adequate to accommodate Clarice Mitchell in modest comfort, might well have been considerable in the eyes of the few people who inhabited it. What surprised her more was that for a period during the succeeding centuries it had become an inn before reverting to a farmhouse. The place was so isolated she wondered where its customers would have come from; it could hardly have relied on passing trade. But, she reminded herself, highways as she recognised them did not exist here even now, and perhaps the track across the high moorland that she had followed was of greater significance in earlier times. She had read in a guidebook that as late as the 1880s men had walked over high commonland to an old homestead for a haircut. So an inn in this remote place might not, after all, be remarkable.

The wind was getting stronger and the light was beginning to thin. She couldn't stay here any longer or she would begin to re-evaluate her insistence that she should be accommodated at the farm, rather than at one of the pubs in the area. She had insisted and that was that. She got out of the car and walked into the farmyard. A woman who was retrieving a small child from what might appear to be an attempt to drown itself in a paddling pool, looked up and said pleasantly, 'Miss Mitchell?'

Two

CLARICE WOKE in the night. She wanted the bathroom but could not think where it was. The position of her bed seemed wrong in relation to the window, which should have been facing her but had now moved alongside. It took longer than it ought to have done to work out where she was. She had been given a room in the middle, and oldest, part of the house with the bathroom adjacent but not *en suite*. The old boards creaked as in a dream of reliving their uprooting when she came into the corridor, and she was thankful that the family slept at the far end of the house. Her bladder certainly needed relieving, but some other pressure remained after she was back in bed and the plumbing had registered a final protest before the house quietened again. This is the aftermath of travel, she told herself, remembering the first night of so many holidays abroad, the feeling of anti-climax and disappointment, the breathtaking scenery not yet on display and the alien beds all too rackingly in evidence.

She lay back and tried to empty her mind, but it wasn't sleep that came. Clarice had prided herself on being a forward-looking person, with the result that the past had not been given enough room in her life. Of late, it had demanded reparation. Certainly, it had begun to occupy her to an irritating extent. Periods of switching off had always been necessary to her, time when she let the mind off its leash and allowed it to go walkabout. Lately, on these occasions the past rushed in like those drivers who must occupy every space on a road. An occasion like this was too good an opportunity for it to miss and in it zoomed to remind her of why she was here.

A woman who had become Rhoda Tresham had been born here in the early part of the last century. Clarice didn't even know her maiden name. In fact, she knew nothing about her except that her granddaughter had been the headmistress of the school Clarice had attended from the age of ten.

All right, all right, she thought wearily, it was a mistake to come here, an impulse I should have resisted. But to no avail. She was already remembering her father, could see him in his hardware store, a cheerful, hard-working man, his non-conformist principles etched into his face. These principles hadn't allowed him to send his cherished only child to a posh school, but he had wanted her to have a better education than he himself had had. The idea of education as the gateway to opportunity and the fulfilled life was tremendously important in her childhood. A determined man, he had obtained from Truman and Knightley a list of girls' independent schools, and over the course of one summer he had visited some fifteen possible candidates for his favour. His method of introduction was unorthodox. He arrived on his bicycle, usually on a Sunday afternoon, travel-stained after a long time in the saddle. His reception ranged from cool to hostile. It was not surprising, therefore, that it was the school at which his advent was greeted without surprise – as if this were an eminently sensible way to set about planning a daughter's education – at which Clarice was enrolled.

A pleasant warmth engulfed Clarice. In retrospect, her schooldays seemed one long summer of ease and happiness. The school was small, no more than seventy boarders who were not unduly inhibited by rules and regulations. Even the timetable was flexible and could be adjusted to accept the gift of a particularly beautiful day or the challenge of a frosty landscape. Whereas most schools aimed at moulding, Miss Wilcox's school broke the mould and worked with and encouraged whatever creature it was who shyly emerged – or, as in Clarice's case, bounced out. Learning was not neglected, only its environment was changed, and within its limits the education was good. The limits set were those of the headmistress herself. She was interested in art, music and the humanities, without which she considered it was not possible to become a fully mature human being; science was not ill-taught, it was simply not taught at all. 'If we can stimulate the mind and feed the imagination, we shan't have failed utterly,' Miss Wilcox was wont to say. She had certainly not failed Clarice, whom she had saved from a life of well-ordered employment and practical good sense and opened the door on the road to grief and pain and joy and longing for the unattainable that is the lot of those who never pitch camp.

So, here I am, Clarice thought, come like a pilgrim to say thank you for releasing my small painterly gift. It wasn't your fault I took so long to free myself from expectation. She saw the old easel in the art room. There was a painting on it; it needed one stroke of colour on the left and as her brush hovered above the palette she fell asleep.

She woke before her alarm went off, which was good, since she drifted gently from sleep and, on the way, her mind alighted in the right place, accepted the strange room and even recalled that a rehearsal had been called for nine-thirty. 'We are very fortunate to have been allocated the theatre in which to rehearse and we must make the most of every minute,' their director had said, severely putting down any suggestion that the first day should be spent exploring the area.

She had breakfast in a room that was also a passage to another room. She could imagine these small inter-connecting areas in the days when the building was an inn. The highbacked bench chair would have fitted in well, as would the long bench that ran the length of one wall, now softened by cushions. Her table was by the window and she could see two toddlers playing on the grass, one hitting the other energetically with a rubber spade. Behind her was a huge fireplace at present filled with dried wild flowers. In an alcove beneath the stairs there was an old chest with an oil lamp on it. The image troubled her imagination.

'Do you know anything about the people who used to farm here?' she asked the young woman who waited on her.

'My husband's family has been here for seventy years.' As long as time was, Clarice thought, looking at the bright face with the lively brown eyes. No point in asking her questions about a long dead family whose name she didn't even know.

She said, 'Perhaps someone would remember one of the granddaughters. She used to visit in the summer holidays – Roberta Wilcox. That would have been as late as the nineteen thirties.'

The pleasant young woman worried as to how to deal tactfully with this idea and Clarice thought, how would I have felt when I was her age if someone had suggested my parents might have remembered Abraham Lincoln?

It seemed however that light had dawned. 'Grandfather kept a diary. I'll ask my mother-in-law to have a look. Roberta Wilcox?'

'I don't want to trouble her. You must be so busy.'

'Oh, she'd love it. She's mad on family history.'

Later, as she was leaving to attend the rehearsal, the farmer's wife came across the yard to say that she would get the diaries out after dinner that night. 'He was very old when I knew him. But every evening, after we'd cleared the table, he used to sit down in the kitchen and write his entry for the day. If there was a disagreement about when something happened locally, people in the village would come to ask him to look it up in the diary.'

They talked with enthusiasm about diaries generally, both, it transpired, being readers not practitioners. Clarice asked, looking at the huddle of outbuildings, 'Which is the theatre?'

The farmer's wife pointed to a long stone barn with a tiled roof standing aloof from the other buildings.

'Do you find it a nuisance, having all these theatre people around?'

'We reckon we're lucky. If you've got to diversify this is the best way as far as we're concerned. And they're a nice crowd, brighten the place up for the young ones. Plays are a bit odd sometimes, but that's the way of things now, isn't it?' She turned away to attend to a child who for some minutes had been proclaiming injury and outrage with increasing volume.

On her way to the theatre Clarice paused at the gate leading into the near field. The sun was bright and she was reluctant to go inside. The director was blocking the first two acts and it seemed a waste of time for her to be there. Across the field she could see a huge shed from which straw, or fodder, was being loaded on to a cart. The sun dazzled her eyes and for a moment the scene shuddered and seemed to shift. She held on to the gate until the dizziness passed. The doctor had warned her against being hard on herself. 'You may get dizzy spells and you must treat them with respect. There is no need for alarm, provided you take sensible precautions.' He had held her eye for a moment and she had realised there was something she had to know. But she preferred to make her own approach, come to it in her own time, not have the moment of acknowledgement dictated by the doctor. So she had thanked him for his advice and had not asked for more information. 'I will try to pace myself,' she had said. Now, remembering this promise, she allowed that she might have pushed herself recently and needed to take things more easily. She turned and walked unhurriedly towards the barn. Above its tiled roof bare hills folded into the horizon. She heard the cry of a bird, thin and high, finishing on a rising note: there was a lure in that cry, an invitation to the hills. A walk in the late afternoon should surely be possible.

The door by which she entered the barn was at the rear of the auditorium. There must be another door on the far side of the building that led immediately backstage, she thought, as she stood accustoming her eyes to the dimness. The air struck chill and she wished she had worn her anorak. She could see figures slouched in the seats, not together as the stage staff might have been, but isolated – actors not at present required, going over words in their heads while they took in the details of the set. Not that there was much detail – an upturned barrel here, a mound there. An actor was seated on one of the barrels. She stopped to listen to him.

'For now the wind begins to blow;
Thunder above, and deeps below,
Make such unquiet, that the ship
Should house him safe is wrackt and split;
And he, good prince, having all lost,
By waves from coast to coast is tost;
All perishen of man, of pelf,
Ne aught escapen but himself;
Till fortune, tired with doing bad,
Threw him ashore, to give him glad:
And here he comes. What shall be next,
Pardon old Gower, – this longs the text.'

The voice was melodious and the actor knew how to ring the changes of mood and emphasis. Although he sat to one side of the stage during the action, his still presence radiated such a benign authority that one never quite forgot he was the story-teller, the players owing their existence to his magic. Alan Meredith had understood the role perfectly from the start and had resisted any temptation to declaim.

Clarice, looking in fond amusement at the sensitive, lantern-jawed face that gained such strength from its assumed role, marvelled once again at the transforming power of theatre. Who would have thought that here was a man who, in daily life, viewed his surroundings with the perplexity of the short-sighted who have never managed to get a proper perspective on the visual world? A man irresolute, indecisive and prone to melancholy, of whom reviewers and adjudicators would comment time and again that he held the stage without effort. Not quite the impression he had created when by some bizarre misjudgement he had been allowed to stand in for one of his Met Office colleagues on the TV weather slot; an occasion on which he had revealed an inability to co-ordinate hand movements and words coupled with a surprising lack of knowledge of the geography of the British Isles. 'You were groping for Southampton in the Moray Firth,' the outraged producer had exclaimed.

Clarice edged towards a door to the right of the stage that she guessed would lead backstage. She found herself on the prompt side and saw a stool placed ready for her.

In the wings on the far side of the stage she could see the wardrobe mistress fitting masks on the followers of Antiochus. The background characters were all to wear masks because the director wanted to capture something of the atmosphere of a Greek play. Some of them were laughing right up to the moment when the mask slipped over their face. Suddenly, they were menacing.

The assistant stage manager had noted her arrival and was coming towards her with a mug of coffee.

'I'm glad it's only the followers who are masked,' Clarice whispered. 'Prompting veiled ladies is bad enough, but a whole company in masks would be impossible.'

'Be a pity to mask your fellow, wouldn't it?' She put the mug in Clarice's hands and padded away.

Clarice thought the pity was that relationships had to be defined, since she had never, in the fifteen years she and Alan Meredith had, loosely speaking, been together, decided exactly what was their relationship. They weren't married and, for reasons of his personality and her need of privacy, they had never set up house together. They had been lovers, but Clarice was old-fashioned enough to find it pathetic that women of her age should speak of their lovers. In any case, they didn't make love very often now. One could understand why some mature couples opted for marriage simply in order to avoid having to explain themselves.

Someone must have slipped into the barn. The door at the rear of the auditorium had been left open and she could see across the cobbled yard a building with half-doors, probably a stable at one time, where another company was rehearsing. In the yard, farm cats stalked unseen prey. It was very still; the light sparking on the cobbles made her feel giddy and for a moment she wasn't quite sure where she was. Then someone shut the door and it was dark. The director said, 'I want to do Scene Two again,' and Pericles began to speak.

Clarice's eyes were by now used to the changes in light.

She saw the group of players on the stage and beyond, in the wings, a black-clad figure climbing a ladder, probably one of the lighting men. Below him, masked faces tilted upwards, not looking as if they were giving him glad. The sense of not knowing where she was persisted. She had always enjoyed that feeling of entering another world once one was back of the stage, but this was different. Hitherto, the mind had managed to hold both worlds, the world of illusion and the real world outside, in balance. She experienced a moment of pure panic.

Clive Geare, who was playing Helicanus, said, 'Don't prompt me, Clarice, love. I want to struggle through this if I can.'

While he struggled she tried to find her place in the script. Surely her attention had wandered for only a matter of seconds, so why did she catch up with him towards the end of the scene?

'Clive Geare has six parts,' Alan Meredith said gloomily as he and Clarice walked on the moor in the late afternoon. 'Six parts! And you know what he can do to a line when he's lost.'

'But he always does it in iambic pentameters,' Clarice pointed out.

Clarice had had in mind a short stroll on the slopes immediately above the farm, but Alan had wanted to see the site of an old mine. Not for the first time their attempts to reconcile the irreconcilable had come to grief. They now found themselves on one of the wilder stretches of the moor. Clarice, looking at the dull, mottled brown expanse dissolving into distance, felt as unforgiving as the scenery and in answer to Alan's tentative, 'It is rather splendid, isn't it?' she answered, 'Well, it certainly echoes those lines, "A thousand ages in Thy sight are like an evening gone." '

She had no difficulty in thinking of those who had shared her evening, lying not too deep below the tussock grass; but it was the earlier people, those who had shared God's afternoon, who crowded in on one here, lying proud in their barrows.

'There would have been more of them than there are people living here now, wouldn't there?' she said, offering an olive branch.

Not surprisingly, he failed to read her mind and replied, 'Good gracious, no! It was only mined for a matter of sixty years.' He was looking into a dark valley where slate-grey water reflected a few stunted trees. 'It has a grim history.' The fact seemed to afford him a melancholy satisfaction that he hoped she might share.

'Well, you can scramble down there if you want to, but I'm staying up here with the Beaker folk.'

She sat on the turf at the path's edge, facing away from that dark declivity towards a hump-backed ridge of dingy green, inset here and there with faint purple.

'Are you feeling all right?' he asked, a little anxious now.

'Let's say I'm not feeling in any need of a grim history. This place is grim enough without that. Do you think there are people who actually like this sort of desolation – misanthropes apart?'

'I quite like it myself,' he said unhappily. 'It doesn't ask anything of one.'

'It doesn't acknowledge one, let alone ask anything. It

was here long before question time.' She closed her eyes. 'It gives me vertigo. I feel like a fly on one of those globes we had in the geography classroom.'

He crouched down beside her. 'That's because it's evening and you're tired.'

'It also reminds me I'm long past my morning.'

He looked at her in helpless dismay and her mood changed. 'Oh, don't fret about it. Go on down and look at your mine. You'll sleep a whole lot better if you've seen your face reflected in its grim history.'

'There's probably an easier way into that valley.'

'I'm sure there is, but not for us. If you don't do it now, we'll only have to come back another time.'

They argued for a while, but in the end he went down. If Alan wanted to do something, he usually did it, however apologetically.

It was a long way down and the way up probably seemed a whole lot longer to him. 'There wasn't anything to be seen,' he said, cross and short of breath. 'It must have been sealed up years ago.'

They were both tired by now and agreed not to meet that evening, which was what Clarice had wanted anyway.

After a substantial meal of roast duck followed by apple pie, Clarice felt sufficiently restored to allow herself a brandy with her coffee. The farmer's wife joined her in the little sitting room set aside for guests.

'This is very kind of you,' Clarice said.

'It's exciting for me – nowadays, it's only members of the family who are interested. She was your headmistress, you say?' They put the television on the floor and gave pride of place to the old leather suitcase that contained the diaries. 'You must have liked her. My headmistress was a tartar; I'd have given a wide berth to the place where she spent her holidays.'

'It isn't curiosity,' Clarice said, moved, as one can be occasionally, to confide in a sympathetic stranger in a way not possible with friends. 'Well, I suppose I was a bit curious. But that came after the decision was made. It was that chance association of the Beacon Theatre and the farm. I don't believe in chance. So I came. I suppose you might say, I'm here to find out why I'm here.'

The farmer's wife seemed unsurprised by this. 'Let's see if we can find something that will help.' She opened the case.

At first sight it looked a formidable task they had set themselves; but the diaries were tied up in decades and Clarice was sure that the most likely months in which there might be references to Roberta Wilcox's visits would be July, August and September. They agreed to take a decade each, the farmer's wife the 1920s and Clarice the 1930s.

It was the farmer's wife who found the first, and longest, entry:

9th July, 1922. A Miss Wilcox called while I was helping Dad with the wagon. She is staying at The Drover. A big lady and most pleasant. She was very interested in the house. It seems her grandmother was born here. She was a Carey. It disappointed her when we said there weren't any Careys farming round here now, it was the Roes farmed here before us. Dad told her the vicar was the one to ask and as I had to fetch the lambs from the heath, I offered to walk the lady there. She told me she was headmistress of a girls' school. You'd not have believed it, she was so jolly. She asked about my brothers and sisters and told me she was one of seven. She was a good, stout walker and when she had seen the vicar she came back to our farm and asked Mother if she could put her up as she means to come back in the spring.

They found the diaries for the spring of the following year. She did come back. There were subsequent references to her throughout the 1920s and early 1930s, but it seemed she became so accepted a visitor that only her arrival was recorded in any detail. She was now a friend of the family and perhaps her original reason for visiting was forgotten in the pleasure of taking part in the life of the farm. From time to time there were glimpses of her riding to sheep sales, raking out the straw in the barns. If ever she found out any more about her grandmother – perhaps during the many conversations she must have had with the womenfolk – it was not recorded.

Most of the entries in the diaries related to events on the farm or in the nearby hamlet of Cherril's Ford and only once in the section that Clarice read did other matters impinge. In 1931 a historical novelist had identified a broken stone pillar, which jutted up at the side of the lane just outside the farm, as the site on which witches had been burnt during the fifteenth century. The old man was sceptical. 'He reckoned there would have been an inscription and wanted to know how long the pillar had been broken. We told him it had been like that ever since we could remember. Anyways, they'd never have bothered with an inscription, not in stone; different if it had been wood, but not something as lasting as stone. Have made it more like a memorial, that would.'

'Do you know the stone?' Clarice asked the farmer's wife.

'Sunk into the earth now, it has; more like a mile post.'

'Do you ever get enquiries about the old priory?'

'From time to time people come asking if we ever dig up any remains in the fields.' She laughed. 'Anything we dig up goes back under pretty quick. We're sitting right over that old priory; the less interest there is in it, the better for us.'

Clarice could understand this attitude. The present grows out of the past's decay; why disturb a natural process? It was eleven o'clock and there must be other matters the farmer's wife had to attend to before she went to bed. Clarice thanked her and they parted, both having enjoyed their time together.

Three

'It's getting old that's my trouble,' Clarice told herself as she was once more plagued by the sense of having lost her bearings. She was sitting in the prompt corner. Around her, different spaces contained seemingly unrelated tableaux — in the wings opposite one of the wardrobe ladies was measuring Alan, tape stretched tight around his chest, disbelief curling her lips in the way that always reminded him he fell short of her ideal of masculinity; in the auditorium the director, a far-away look in his eyes, was pretending to listen to the lighting man; while on stage Pericles was recounting how, accompanying the barmaid from the pub the previous evening, his amorous advances had been brought to an abrupt end by a close encounter with a moorland pony.

I am in some kind of no-man's-land, Clarice thought. Age is a foreign country, and the old are like people who must live far from home, the place which has been left behind is ill-remembered and, even could it be revisited, would occasion shock and dismay. And the future? Could it be that the future is more friendly — like a room in a house that you haven't yet been into, but you know it's there, furnished, with every appearance of being lived in, and when you do walk into it, you'll have a sense of recognition?

She had had something of that feeling when she first entered the farmhouse, not so much the sense of having been there before, but of a place waiting for her.

The director, for whom everyone had been waiting, suddenly said in an exasperated tone, 'Can we make a start now, please?'

Pericles pretended not to hear and went on with his saga. 'Carver Doone and the Hound of the Baskervilles rolled into one!'

The director said, 'Now, please,' at his most intimidating, and Antiochus whispered to Pericles, 'What of the wench, though – Jamaica?' and everyone on stage let loose their frustrations in a blare of laughter.

The director, aware that however puerile he might find this display there was nothing he could do about it, said, 'Perhaps we should have coffee now, Liz, since everyone seems so unsettled.'

Pericles said gloomily to Clarice as they waited for the milk jug to be handed round, 'We're all going to be kept in during the lunch break now.'

She was looking over his shoulder, frowning.

'What is it?' he asked.

'I thought the company that's rehearsing in the stables were doing The Crucible.'

'So I heard.'

'Then their wardrobe people haven't got a very good sense of period.'

He turned to look in the direction she had been looking. The door at the rear of the auditorium had swung open, but whoever Clarice had seen had moved away.

'Don't really want them looking in on us, do we?' he

said, not taking kindly to the idea that his foolery had been witnessed by a member of a rival company. He edged past the jostle of people around the coffee tray and closed the door.

Clarice, who noted and deplored a growing tendency in herself to defend not only her own, but others' privacy, was discouraged by the effect the intrusion had had on her. There was no doubt she was becoming worse. She would soon be as territorial as her old Border terrier, Maggie, who had resented anyone coming near Clarice's car and had on one occasion petrified an innocent group of children on a beach who had presumed to approach the spot where she was guarding Clarice's clothes. But lecture herself as she might, the agitation remained and several times during the morning she glanced towards the door at the rear of the auditorium.

In the afternoon, just when she felt more relaxed and was enjoying Pericles's playing of the shipwreck scene, the woman came again. She stood in the doorway, the light behind her, quite still. How long she stayed Clarice did not know because the director began to tell them about cuts he was making and, by the time she had amended her script, the woman had gone.

Clarice said, 'Do you think we could have that door bolted? It keeps swinging open.' She was reluctant to mention the woman until she was more in possession of herself.

'I'm not sure one can have a barn door bolted,' the director said, annoyed at the interruption.

'It's a theatre now.' Clarice was unrepentant. 'It's not full of straw.'

Antiochus, edgily determined to be flippant, said, 'But we hope it will soon be full of people.'

'Will someone please shut the bloody door so that we can get on with this rehearsal,' the director said in his quiet, I-am-at-breaking-point voice.

The woman came once more towards evening and again she stood quite still, looking towards the stage. Well-to-do, mid-Victorian, Clarice thought, seeing the outline of the dress, the suggestion of lace at throat and cuffs, certainly not Puritan New England. She resolved that tomorrow she herself would take matters in hand.

But in the morning it was different. The woman must have entered by the backstage door because, without warning, she appeared in the wings and, gathering her skirts above her ankles, walked across the stage and paused for a moment in front of the prompt corner, before making her exit. The actors took no notice; but actors became astonishingly resigned to infringements of their space − lighting staff bearing ladders, stage management marking the position of furniture, sound staff checking positioning of speakers. The director, who could at times block out anything he did not wish to see, or hear, or know, went on with the rehearsal as if nothing had happened. Clarice, mouth dry and heart pounding with rage, could barely wait for the morning break to tackle the stage manager.

'I think it's a bit much for a member of one of the other companies to come prowling around in here while we're rehearsing.'

'I don't know what you're talking about,' he said impatiently.

'Well, we don't want them to see it until we're ready, do we? She could be reporting on what we're doing, or not doing.' She could feel her cheeks flushed with agitation.

'What is this all about?'

'The tall woman in Victorian costume, you must have seen her, she's an arresting enough figure, and she walked right across . . .'

'There are so many people scrambling in and out of costumes, I'm not surprised if an odd Victorian has crept in! Do you know how many parts Mike Lewis is playing? Five, and you know how long it takes to get him into one costume. And the wardrobe people can't do it in the changing rooms because it's got to be done so quickly. So it's all happening right here.' Seeing her troubled face, he calmed down and put an arm around her shoulders. 'I'm sorry, love, but just don't add to my problems; you're usually such a trouble-free prompter.'

'Yes, all right.'

'Tell me if she does it again and I'll tackle her.'

But Clarice knew that she would not tell him.

They worked through lunch. The rehearsal went well and the director called it a day at half-past three.

Pericles said that his friend the barmaid worked during the daytime in a tea-room and the theatre emptied rapidly, even the director being drawn by the promise of food.

'Maybe she's not so keen since you mistook her for a pony,' Antiochus said as they went out.

'No, no, she's a great lass. Wonderful sense of humour.'

Their voices died away. Alan had been well to the fore; he would not notice Clarice's absence for some time. He wouldn't give it much thought, knowing from long experience how it irritated her to have to stop for tea.

She sat on the prompt stool and waited, looking towards the door at the back of the auditorium. The effort it took to sit there quietly was surprising; one might almost have thought it required courage. The company had left the door open. There was a farm truck in the yard which blocked the light so that the doorway became an empty frame. Presently, the woman came and filled it. For a long time the two women looked at each other, the strange woman seeming as interested in Clarice's costume – the rumpled jersey and corduroy slacks – as was Clarice in hers. Then Clarice got up and descended the steps at the side of the stage. The woman watched her advance until she was half-way down the auditorium, then she turned into the yard. Clarice followed. Her eyes watched the lavender grey dress so intently that she did not notice where the woman was leading her. It was certainly not to the stable block where *The Crucible* was in rehearsal, for the set on which she eventually found herself was definitely Victorian. And rather well done, Clarice grudgingly admitted, as her eyes took in the clutter of furniture and the numerous pictures on the walls. The property department must have been both well informed and hard-working to have assembled all this. Then she caught sight of a face in a mirror. Close curled grey hair framed wry, puzzle-wrinkled features: her own face, oddly incongruous in this period setting. Her gaze turned down stage and her heart missed a beat. She was looking at a fourth wall. This was not a stage set, it was a sitting room. In fact, it was the small sitting room in which only yesterday she and the farmer's wife had sat reading the

33

diaries of an old man who would not have been born at the time this room was furnished.

The woman was standing by the window, a little to one side, as if she did not wish to be seen looking out. Was she wondering if she had been followed? Because of her slanting stance, Clarice could see her clearly for the first time. Her face had the clarity of a freshly cleaned painting. Quite a few of her kind must have looked out of old gilt frames, their eyes seeming to reflect on something outside the viewer's range. Her skin was pale with the faintest touch of pink on cheeks and lips. Clarice noticed how the thick eyebrows gave definition to the face, perfectly complementing the eyes that might otherwise have seemed enigmatic. Put those eyebrows on a face less harmoniously proportioned and you'd have a clown, she thought, whereas what you've got is a haughty English rose.

The woman turned away, apparently satisfied, and sat at a small desk in the corner to the side of the window. She took a key from the pocket of her dress, unlocked a drawer and drew out a small leather-cased book. At first, Clarice thought she meant to read, but suddenly she reached forward and took a pen from the ledge at the front of the desk. After a moment's reflection, she dipped the pen in the brass inkwell and began to write.

Even if I die for this, Clarice thought, and it didn't seem too unlikely a consequence at that moment, I must find out what it is she's writing. She moved quietly forward and, holding her breath, looked over the woman's shoulder.

The writing was small but legible and Clarice read:

Today I saw the strange woman again. For I am sure this poor ghost is, in fact, a woman. It is true she is dressed as a man, though no man I ever saw dressed in quite this fashion; and the grey hair is cut close, a crop of little curls that would spring back into place after they are brushed, just like a child's. But the face is a woman's face. It is so alive, this little monkey face, so full of interest, and the eyes look at me with such warmth . . .

Four

SINCE I first saw her, I have followed her into the barn that seems to have some significance for her. She sits there on a stool with a book in her lap, a lamp to one side of her that throws an eerie light. She seems intent on some scene that is hidden from me.

Why have they come to me, my two ghosts? It would be such a relief could I disclose their presence, but were I to confide in Edward, he would be very distressed. He would think it a sign of that ill-health he so dreads in me, without any idea that he himself fosters it. He would fear for my mind. If only I could make him understand that there is nothing to fear save fear itself.

Rhoda Tresham had laid the pen down while she sought for something she could not quite put into words. But it was not a sudden intellectual enlightenment that focused the eyes and brought colour to her cheeks, it was the barking of dogs and the sound of heavy footsteps in the yard. One glance out of the window and the book was quickly thrust into the drawer. The ghosts, it would seem, were locked away with it and her animated attention bestowed on the new arrival, now being greeted in the yard by her husband. As she watched the two men, her colour came and went as unaffected eagerness disputed with a more sober propriety.

'You are most welcome,' Edward Tresham was saying as the two men walked towards the farmhouse. 'But you will have to make do with my wife and myself, for the family is off at the horse fair.' As they entered the house, he called out, 'The vicar is come, my dear.'

The newcomer, stooping slightly as he crossed the threshold, murmured a civil reply. His was a strong presence. It was not merely the mud-splattered clothes that brought the smell of peat bog into the house and reminded one of his exertions; there was an energy released around him, the thrust of an on-going journey. He was a man of contradictions, sensuality apparent in the mouth and the droop of the eyelids, but a little quivering of a nerve in the cheek suggesting sensitivity, even vulnerability. Perhaps aware of how his abrasiveness contrasted with Mrs Tresham's ivory delicacy, he seemed ill at ease in her presence and had some difficulty in striking the right note in his greeting. He looked as though he were still outside, a traveller glimpsing through a window a symbol of domesticity his travels unfitted him to share. His manner was unaccountably reserved when he apologised for imposing on her time.

'No,' Edward assured him. 'We are most anxious to hear the news you bring. My wife will be much eased in mind to learn that things are not so bad as she had feared.'

As there had been no time for the clergyman to impart his news, this was a strange statement, revealing some anxiety in the speaker, as though by using this form of words he might hold at bay, if not actually avert, some calamity. His companion, more inclined to meet calamity head on, replied tersely, 'I bring no good news, I'm afraid.'

Edward Tresham immediately turned to his wife. 'My dear, I think it might be best . . .'

'It would be best were we to allow Mr Jory to be seated after his long walk,' she replied. 'Millie has kept a good fire in the parlour.'

Millie had been coming and going all the afternoon to Edward's irritation, this, in his view, being no way for a servant to behave. Now, no sooner were they seated and had exchanged a few necessary courtesies, than the old woman bustled in unbidden, carrying a loaded tray. 'When I saw you come, I said to myself, Parson will be wanting good food inside him after tramping the moor.'

'You spoil me, Millie.' He spoke as one more familiar with the ways of the household than either of his present companions; and, since they were the guests of a few weeks, he was not unduly concerned to avoid Edward's displeasure.

Rhoda Tresham, aware that given encouragement the old woman would make one of the party, hovering in the background and constantly interposing her opinions, went to help her lay out the tea things. Edward watched his wife. He had the fastidious, finely wrought features of the perfectionist and there was about him that sense of strain felt by those for whom every object must be held in its right place, every thought examined so that no loose ends are left lying about: a man who perceived the crust of civilisation to be very thin. His gaze betrayed the delicate balance of his peace. His wife's fragility was both a torment and a necessity to him; failing health could rob him of his dearest treasure, yet were she to become more robust, the danger might be the greater. The other man watched him, the twist of his lips suggesting he might understand a little more than Edward Tresham would have found comfortable.

'I will look after this now, Millie,' Rhoda said gently. 'My husband wishes to speak to Mr Jory.' She contrived, while making the dismissal unequivocal, to suggest that the whims of menfolk must be humoured.

'Oh, I know what he come about,' the old woman said in a penetrating whisper. 'And 'tis my opinion that little mite never left home alive.' At the door, she made her final pronouncement. 'When I was a young girl, they'd not have wasted no court's time dealing with him.'

'My dear,' Edward looked at his wife with tender concern when tea and scones had been plentifully dispensed. 'I think this may be painful . . . '

Rhoda, apparently having no mind to be spared, seated herself and said, 'What is your view of this matter, Mr Jory?'

'As you know, Jarvis's story is that he left the cottage with the little maid before morning light, to take her to live with his sister in Mellor.'

'I suppose there is still a chance she is with this sister?' Edward said.

'But how would he have communicated his intention to the sister, an unlettered man?' Rhoda asked.

Edward waved this aside. 'I doubt these people worry about such things. They are feckless and don't think ahead. He probably arrived with the child . . . '

'And what arrangements did he make for the other children to be cared for in his absence? Feckless he may be, but he surely wouldn't abandon them.'

It was Jory who answered. 'People's memories are not always reliable, but the cottagers, who are the only folk likely to have noticed his movements, think he was not gone long enough to have travelled to Mellor and back – that, at least, is what they now believe to be the case. As for the children, they are with Mrs Oldman for the time being.' There was a pause while they let these facts settle in their minds, then Jory said, 'But to acquaint you with the latest development – young Rob Simpson, out searching for a dog that had attacked his sheep, came across the remains of a fire and when he kicked over the ashes he found a buckle and pieces of burnt cotton print. I took Mrs Tibbs up there today and she has identified the cotton as part of little Ellie's pinafore.'

Edward, aghast, held up his hand, signalling that no more be said, but Jory went on, 'Nothing else. No human remains were found.'

There was a heavy silence, then Jory said, 'The first thing to do, of course, is to see the sister. I plan to set out for Mellor tomorrow.'

Rhoda said, 'I pray that you may find the little girl there, safe and well; but there seems scant hope.'

'It is hard to believe such wickedness.' Edward Tresham was deeply affected. He looked out of the window as if some explanation might lie outside among those bleak hills. 'This is a rough, harsh place – I am afraid you had forgotten just how harsh, my dear.' He seemed to feel a need to underline this statement by explaining to Jory, 'As you know, my wife was born on this farm and passed her childhood here. The childhood vision is very selective and she sees this place as a lost paradise, especially the moor. Yes, yes, you do, my dear. I just hope that this terrible crime will correct that image and you will no longer wish to make these yearly visits to stay with your cousin.'

'Here at least what happens is known to us,' Jory said crisply. 'In London there must be terrible crimes committed of which you are quite unaware.'

'But is it not better to be unaware, if there is nothing we can do to mend matters?' Edward turned to Rhoda. 'I know you don't agree with me, my dear.' She made no reply and he went on, talking to Jory as though she were no longer there. 'My wife, you see, thinks that knowledge will work miracles. She is intent on sending our daughter to this new school that Miss Beale has founded.'

'Is your daughter then in need of a miracle?' Jory had an uncomfortable way of pruning a conversation to the quick and Edward was disconcerted. But it was not Edward at whom he was looking.

Rhoda said quietly, 'I think education helps people to understand their world and it gives them the ability to change their lives.' She allowed her eyes to meet his; the look was held for a length of time she could only regard as audacious.

They were both shaken by the force of something exchanged, unmediated by words. Jory looked into the heart of the fire, his face reflecting its ruddy glow. Rhoda poured hot water into the teapot. Her hand was unsteady and the water splashed across her knuckles; the pain steadied her, indeed she welcomed it.

Edward was saying, 'There has been some fear expressed that a woman's brain and health would suffer if exposed to the rigorous intellectual training to which boys are subjected. Indeed, I have heard one eminent doctor say that he seriously considers it might damage the reproductive system.' He would not normally have made such a comment in mixed society, but he was very agitated. He gazed at his wife as she bent forward to fill his cup, her face so prettily flushed by the firelight, and he thought how readily this sweet, rosy bloom might turn to fever. 'Then, also, there is the contact with pupils from the lower orders – because this, it seems, is what is intended; and this contamination, for this is what I am afraid it would be, could only have the worst possible consequences. I know that you have taken an interest in providing education for the poorer classes. What is your opinion?'

Jory, who had not attended to this speech, said, 'That I must set out again. There are pressing church matters I must see to if I am to leave for Mellor tomorrow.'

Rhoda's relatives returned soon after he had left. The children played in the yard, the Treshams' daughter, Veronica, among them. The farmer, Harold, and his wife, Rhoda's cousin Eleanor, were eager to hear the news that Jory had brought, but Rhoda excused herself, saying they would understand that she could not bear to hear this tale twice told.

Indeed, there was much that she could not bear. Upstairs in the bedroom, she composed herself to pray for the lost child. Mr Jory had said she should pray for the father, too, which had angered Edward, who had retorted,

'I do not agree that we are not called upon to judge; surely, we are daily called upon to make judgements, the choice between good and evil is never made once and for all, but it sometimes seems to me is presented to us almost hourly.' To this, Rhoda could only say amen.

After a time she grew calmer and listened to the children chanting in the yard. '. . . a bunch of blue ribbon to tie up my hair'. She had the sense of time running through her fingers. The light was failing and a voice called the children in. Someone was still singing. It was not the voice of someone singing out of doors; there was an echo, as there might be in a church.

> '. . . a length of green say,
> I asked him to bring me
> A length of green say.'

Five

CLARICE HAD known several people who claimed to have seen ghosts. Those of her friends who had had what might be termed paranormal experiences were admirably matter-of-fact about them and the one person who owned to a resident ghost – a gardener, not a living-in one – seemed to be on good terms with it and happy to let it roam at will among her flower borders. They all testified to the benignity of these apparitions. 'There is nothing in the least frightening about them.' Had it been otherwise, their manner suggested, they would not have tolerated the intrusion.

Clarice was far less nonchalant. As she saw it, either something was very wrong with the generally accepted laws of nature, or Clarice Mitchell was suffering from some abnormality, a dysfunction of the brain. Throughout the remainder of the day she had been unable to think of anything but that unnerving description of herself, written by a woman who had lived a century earlier. The feeling grew that she was cut off from the people around her, the theatre groups, the farmworkers; even the sight of the postman on his bicycle gave her a sense of immense isolation. 'She's becoming more and more neurotic,' she had said only recently to Alan, referring to one of the wardrobe assistants who was plagued by a ghost whose delight it was to come in during the night and rearrange all the costumes that had been carefully hung in the order in which they were required. No one, as far as she knew, had produced a ghost who made notes about them in a day book. Her mind worried away at the events of the last few months, trying to identify other instances of instability, to pin down what it was that had triggered her decline. She had had trouble with a painting, but that was an occupational hazard long since accepted. Physically, she noted more signs of wear and tear. These, too, she accepted; she was coming up to seventy and would soon be living in injury time. Perhaps the oddest thing that had happened had been her decision to come here.

In the middle of the night it came to her that she must find the diary. Perhaps the desk was still there, pushed away into a corner of that cluttered sitting room. She got up and, pulling on her dressing gown, tiptoed on to the landing. All was quiet and she remembered that no one else was sleeping in this part of the house. She switched on the hall light which should be sufficient to enable her to see what she was doing.

There was a desk in the sitting room, but she thought it was too large and heavy to be the one at which the woman had seated herself. Even so, she pulled open the drawers. The small top ones at either side were stuffed with old snapshots and farm catalogues; the lower, larger ones contained a table-tennis net, ping-pong balls, lead toy soldiers and an assortment of jigsaw puzzles. It had been a ridiculous notion. The sensible thing would be to ask the farmer's wife whether, by any chance, pieces of the Carey family's furniture remained in the house. But how would that help? If she failed to find the diary, it proved nothing. The possibility that she might find it was unthinkable; a fact emphasised by the queasiness of her stomach.

And then, going up the stairs, she recalled seeing other words written in the diary; other words which, so fascinated had she been by the description of herself, she had overlooked. 'Why have they come to me, my *two* ghosts?' Two. Not a little personal matter then, between herself and this woman. Her heart stalled; a small tremor seemed to shake the house. This is the thing I have been warned of, she thought, kneeling on the stairs. In the hall mirror she could see her face framed by the banister rails, as people sometimes say they see ghosts, staring through bars or a palisade as if looking out from another dimension. For some time she clung there, too faint to move, cold sweat soaking her nightdress. In time, the machinery of her body started up again, albeit grudgingly. She hauled herself up to the landing, resting on each tread, and finally, leaning on the wall for support, reached her bedroom. She took a pill and lay down in her dressing gown, drawing the duvet over her shivering limbs. The room swayed, and the bed swayed up and down, not unpleasantly, had one not known this was not its natural motion. Accompanying this sensation of being rocked was an odd distortion of vision. Beyond the window, the moonlight seemed to throw the shadow of a great wall across the yard and into the field. It was as though she were looking out of the window of a building many times larger than the farm. As she looked, the light changed and grew brighter. Her hand rested on the window-sill and as she felt the sun's warmth spread up her arm, she went to sleep like a comforted child.

Six

A YOUNG WOMAN of some sixteen years, sitting on the sill of the priest's room in the priory, felt the warmth of the sun on her flesh and found it more difficult than usual to collect her thoughts. She pushed the tawny hair back from her forehead, her fingers groping among the curls as she teased out more words.

'And say to him that I hope he will not forget the cinnamon, for I have tried everywhere and cannot get it here. And I hope he keeps well, for we hear reports of sickness in the towns. And to buy, if he can, a length of say of that green he so much admired in my sister-in-law's gown. And I hope he will be with us soon.'

The quill scratched the parchment, translating Joan Mosteyn's hopes into a sinister pattern of black characters. The nuns' priest looked at what he had penned and said, 'Written at Foxlow Priory on this twentieth day of September, 1460 in the reign of Henry the Sixth . . . Do you understand that may not be the case, Joan?' She did not understand. He explained, 'It is said that Richard, Duke of York, has landed in Cheshire and means to claim the throne.' And much Joan cared about that, so long as her husband returned soon.

The priest said, 'I have business to attend to, so I will walk part of the way with you.'

Outside, the wind was strong and it billowed the girl's gown and whipped her cheeks scarlet. 'There is no need for you to come to me if you wish to send another letter,' the priest told her, as they walked along the track leading to the village. 'I will come to you, if you send for me.'

'I like to come,' she answered. Her mother was staying with her and an excuse to escape was welcome. Her mother had told her only that morning, 'You're well enough to look at and there's no serious fault in you, you're honest and ready to please; but once the bloom fades you'll have little to commend you to a husband. You're scatter-brained, idle, and a bad manager.'

Above, the clouds raced across the sky and the wind tore at the thorns in the thicket. The tumult touched a nerve in the girl's body and she wanted to throw back her head and laugh. Everything around her was alive and dancing, only woman must go about her business soberly. If the priest had not accompanied her, she would have tossed her cloak aside and danced like the madwoman who came to the village last spring.

The priest, frowning at the dust rising from the track beneath their feet, said, 'I trust you are taking advantage of your husband's absence to order the house well?'

'It's more difficult than I had thought,' she said resentfully. 'I hadn't expected the servants would need so much attention.' It had not occurred to her that instruction would be necessary; servants, she had imagined, not only did things, but knew what things to do and when and how. 'I'm to supervise the weaving of household clothing, plan the winter supplies, the salting and the pickling, and see that we have sufficient food to meet the needs of wayfarers. I sometimes feel it would be less trouble were I to do the work myself.' And that was saying a lot, because she did not like work.

'You must make sure they realise you are indeed their mistress,' the priest told her severely. 'It is not a matter of their carrying out your instructions, you must make sure that the work is well done.'

'So I begin to see.'

'And you must study the art of being thrifty and frugal, while still maintaining a good table.'

Joan nodded and pulled at a plant struggling to break free of the thorns; she crushed the leaf between her fingers to see whether it smelt pleasant.

'Otherwise the servants will not respect you.'

'You would think they would be pleased to have a mistress who did not ask too much of them, wouldn't you?' she said wistfully. Her standards of order and cleanliness were not exacting, but instead of working with a will because she was so easy to satisfy, the servants grew daily more lackadaisical. She told the priest something of this and he assured her that if only she would set her mind to it, she would succeed because the management of a household was a natural function of a woman.

She listened and said optimistically, 'Well, if it's natural, I expect I shall come to it in time.'

She hoped it would be soon rather than late, since it was something Martin expected of her and she wanted to please him. She wanted to please him in other ways, too. She had not had much joy of her wedding night, and even on subsequent nights when her husband was sober she had not had quite the pleasure she had anticipated. She

49

hoped that would come soon, too. She earnestly desired pleasure.

After they parted company, she walked down a steep track to a deep pool, so bound about by bushes and stunted trees that the water was always still. A magic pool, it was said, where wishes would be granted. She knelt down and looked into it, but was so taken by the face that gazed up at her she forgot to wish; a broad face gashed by a wide mouth split open to laughter and encompassed by a cloud of abundant tawny hair shot with darker strands of chestnut.

'Oh,' she cried, 'but I was comely then.'

'She has been maundering all the morning,' Dame Ursula said to the prioress, looking with disfavour at the woman for whom their charity was demanded. In spite of all efforts to promote cleanliness and order, she still looked as if she had been dragged through a thorn bush backwards; her hair a thicket through which eyes that were surprisingly bright surveyed the scene, like an animal deciding whether to come out of cover, her clothes a bundle of faded rags.

'She may be maundering, but she is working at the same time, and her stitching is improving.' To the prioress's mind, being able to do two things at once denoted a certain intelligence, particularly when one of those things involved somewhat complex forays into the past.

Dame Ursula, who found the creature a sore trial, ventured to say, 'Her wits are so addled I doubt she ever knows where she is at any one moment.'

The prioress correctly interpreted this as a hint that it

was of little advantage for the creature to be here at Foxlow Priory. She said, as she had said before, 'God has sent her to us to look after.'

The prioress had a strong, intelligent face and a manner that, ever since she was a girl, had conveyed the impression that she saw much around her that could be re-ordered with advantage. She was a woman possessed of great powers. When she first entered the priory in 1473 she had hoped that in this closed world of women she would have the opportunity to exercise these powers. Twelve years had gone by and her hopes had not been entirely realised; she felt cramped at Foxlow. The advent of the madwoman had been welcome to her: a challenge with which she might confront her nuns and shake them out of their complacency.

When the madwoman had appeared one morning, dancing down the village street and shrieking curses at any who ventured near her, the villagers had run to the priory for help. Prioress Winifred, who had advanced ideas, allowed her nuns to go outside on errands of mercy 'for so many others go outside on worldly missions, it were a pity for the good to hold back'. When the appeal came, therefore, she sent Dame Priscilla and Dame Ursula to observe the unhappy creature.

The madwoman was a fearsome sight. At first glance, she appeared to be of more than normal stature, but this impression was due to the wild mass of hair that made her seem at least a foot taller, while the odd twigs and foliage that festooned her person added to her girth. She jigged about in her ragged clothes and flapped her arms like a flightless bird.

The two nuns stood with gravely folded hands and wondered whatever they were to do. The madwoman advanced cautiously, like a wary animal, head to one side. Dame Ursula closed her eyes, but Dame Priscilla, her flat face peering from her cowl like a little owl, sensed that there was no need of fear. The madwoman halted within three feet of the nuns; she folded her hands and closed her eyes. She found this mimicry excessively funny. Her lips trembled and tears ran down her face; she bent over, hands clutching her stomach, and laughed so violently that Dame Ursula thought she must rupture herself. Dame Priscilla, however, had the strange experience of feeling that she had entered into the madwoman; she too had danced down the street only to find herself confronted by two strange creatures dressed all in grey with solemn faces and piously folded hands. She began to laugh and at this the madwoman stretched out her hands towards Dame Priscilla. Then, as the nun moved forward, she stepped back, and so they proceeded step by step down the street until poor Dame Ursula thought they would walk off the edge of the earth leaving her to face the villagers and the angry prioress. She decided she had no option but to join this strange procession.

They came to the end of the village where the street petered out into a small copse; here the madwoman stopped. Her gaiety dropped from her, as though it were a mask she had cast aside. Her stripped face was so desolate that Dame Ursula shivered, but Dame Priscilla said bravely, 'My child' (which was absurd for she was the younger by many years), 'tell us your trouble.'

The woman said in a voice soft as the rustle of dry

leaves, 'They have taken my children. My children have been killed.'

Dame Priscilla stepped back, her courage unequal to venturing into the wood if there were children but lately murdered there.

But the woman's mood had changed again, and now she looked about her in bewilderment. 'I know not how I came here.'

All the life had gone from her and Dame Priscilla was able to lead her docilely down the village street and through the priory gates.

'It is God's will that she should find peace,' the prioress had pronounced. 'He has sent her to us and we must care for her.'

They allowed her to stay in a niche in the outer wall of the chapel, little bigger than a kennel, where long ago an anchoress had lived. She seemed to settle there. When the fit was not on her, she was no trouble to anyone. Now, she was singing as she stitched. 'A length of green say, I asked him to bring me a length of green say.'

'Hush,' Dame Ursula admonished.

'But I'm singing to my lady.'

'That is blasphemous.'

'She come to me, my lady comes to me. She's very beautiful and she has a long lavender robe and it shimmers ever so slightly when she moves. She makes a record of me in a book; I see her look into my eyes and then she writes my thoughts in the book.'

Dame Ursula made the sign of the cross. Surely this image of the Holy Virgin making notes about the thoughts of such as Joan Mosteyn would convince the prioress that she had made a mistake in bringing the creature into the priory. She found the prioress's expression hard to read.

Seven

THE SMALL cove was deserted, most people having decided it was too cold for sitting on the sand. There were no bathers – this jagged, rock-strewn coast delivered its own warning only too effectively – but a continuous trickle of people made their way to where, at the foot of the rocks, a path curved out beyond the promontory into the next bay. Carrying babies, wheeling push-chairs, leading dogs, in high-heeled sandals, slacks, cardigans, old and young, they clambered on to the path, walking past the sign that said, 'This path is covered by the incoming tide'. Children explored the caves in the massive cliffs or paddled in the pools left over from the last tide, emerging joyfully covered in green slime.

'What will happen to them?' Clarice asked the old man who had lit his pipe and was settling down for one of the few remaining entertainments provided free.

'They'll come back, squeaking and squawking, those that didn't get too far; those that go right round into the next bay will find there's no way out there and they'll come scrambling back, cross about spoiling their shoes. Some of the ones that climbed'll maybe get up on the headland, though it's all of seven hundred foot, so they'll need to know what they're about – others'll just have to wait.' He chuckled over his reminiscences of the unfortunate. 'Notice is clear enough; ain't nobody they can sue.'

Beneath the cliffs, rocks lay strewn across the cove, many weathered smooth; here and there little islands of sand remained. Clarice could see that it was possible to walk out across the rocks to where the sea was coming in with every appearance of leisure, flicking out an occasional foam-coated tongue and then retreating as if it had changed its mind. She reckoned she would be safe out there provided she watched the danger spots where a sudden inrush might be made.

'You see that reef,' the old man pointed, reading her mind. Clarice located the reef, a long line of rock gnarled as an old tree trunk with a bit chipped out in the middle. 'Once that gap's breached, tide'll come in fast.'

It was twelve o'clock, two hours since she had announced that she needed a day off. The director had been too dumbfounded by the boldness of this assertion to argue. Undoubtedly, it was the only day off she could hope for, so the best use must be made of it, she told herself sternly, as she began to make wary progress, her eye on an island of sand around which the sea was already moving stealthily. She soon found that she could manage perfectly well, and, pleased at her agility, stepped easily from one rock to another. For a moment, when she reached her goal, she felt exhilarated. Boulders formed a circle round the patch of sand, turning it into a miniature cove; she found a rock with a little hollow in the centre, folded up her anorak, and sat on it. She ate sandwiches, drank coffee from the flask provided by the farmer's wife, and watched the beached boats that waited for the water to lift them. After a while, she had to climb on to a higher boulder a little nearer the shore. Around her the sea gently, almost imperceptibly, explored its familiar channels. She thought that further out one rock might have disappeared, but the reef was still there, the gap unbreached, water lying smooth as glass on either side of it.

She reflected.

It had been necessary to get away. This business with the ghosts had been a shock, a salutary reminder that things had been moving out of true for some little while, and there was something in the atmosphere of the house itself, a disturbance she had never expected to feel again, that compounded her unease. She needed time away to consider. It might well be necessary to leave with apologies all round; plead poor health, humiliating though that might be. She was, after all, no stranger to humiliation. But to decide one must clear the mind, break the obsessive rhythm that takes over in times of stress.

Somewhere on her journey to the farm, the sensible, no-nonsense Clarice whom she had presented to the outer world for the last twenty-five years – her up-front woman – had finally slipped away and now she seemed to stand at some distance, like a figure on the shore watching as a ship moves out to sea . . . Clarice tasted salt on her lips; the little wind stirred up by the incoming tide fingered her hair, not like the wind on the moor, tearing on its way somewhere else, but a small, personal caress, intimate and teasing. She experienced that feeling of the sea within her that can come after the first plunge when one gives oneself into this other element, a loosening and shifting as taut muscles relax.

What was it she had intended? To clear her mind, free it from the obsessive rhythm, that was it, was it? She laughed aloud and rested her head on her knees. She had actually come here, of all places, to get away from ghosts! If it had been a mistake to come to the moor, it had been an even greater mistake to come to the sea. Or, viewed from another angle, she raised her head and looked beyond the bay to the open sea, a natural progression. It depended on which way you thought you were travelling.

One summer she had taken a cottage on an island in the Hebrides, and he, Robert Havelock, the only significant he in her life, had joined her there. It was a risk, but they had got away with it. Not that she had cared about risk by then, but it mattered to him. He had more to lose; while she had no reservations, had nothing that she withheld from him. She travelled light at that time, free of all constraints. A college friend, one of the two people who knew of their affair, had told her she was mad. 'You've landed a plum headship and now you start an affair with one of the governors! And you know who will suffer if you're found out. He might have to resign as a governor, but that won't cost him much. It's always the woman who pays.'

But what had payment to do with this joy that filled her life? Whether the situation was fair on her – or on his wife, for that matter – was irrelevant, a question she had never considered. Her friend told her she had lost her pride, and perhaps she had; but it seemed she had found a better kind of pride, a pride and a pleasure in giving. Never had she held her head so high, or her eye been so bright and challenging. The friend said she was wanton, and if showering all one's blessings on a loved one was wanton, if that was what it was to be wanton, then she was wanton. Nor had she ever regretted it.

He was the one who was more torn and she had loved him for that, loved him for the conscience that tormented him and the weakness that made him unable to live up to his own ideals. He never excused himself; that she would have despised.

Now, with every gentle thrust of the sea, he came back to her, with each soft, ingenious infiltration, he moved within her again. It wasn't even a coming back; this was not the past recollected in tranquillity, this was the past happening within the present.

While the sea made its inroads she experienced again the whole of her love affair with Robert Havelock, as if it had been crystallised in concentrated form, waiting this moment when the crust should be broken. When she looked at the wavering rocks now covered by water, his face surfaced like a blurred image in a crowd suddenly clarified in close up. He was there before her as he had been at the stuffy governors' meeting when their eyes met in that look of complete understanding that can suddenly surprise two strangers. Afterwards, it seemed that the whole of their love and their parting had been made known to her in that moment. Certainly she had always realised she would lose him, though she had no foreknowledge of the way of it.

She liked a man to be strong and sure of what he believed, even if she didn't agree with him. In this, Robert had resembled her father, and he, too, was influenced by his background. Underlying his gentle courtesy and his unfailing consideration for others, was the fierce loyalty of the clan. It was loyalty rather than principle that touched the deepest chords in him, though she had not at first understood that. His concern for the feelings of his tiresome wife she had respected, seeing in it the expression of the gentler side of his nature. He had married a woman of great beauty and scant intelligence; with the passage of the years the beauty had faded and a certain stubborn stupidity had replaced what had once appeared as airy inconsequentiality. He bore his disappointment with patience and good humour, aware that the initial error of judgement was his. This mixture of strength and gentleness in him overwhelmed Clarice. He, who could be so resolute, would go to infinite trouble to avoid giving unnecessary pain, and over inessentials he was always ready to give way. He had a long patience that she envied. Combative to a degree, ready to waste energy debating a trifle, Clarice had learnt much from Robert Havelock that had been of invaluable help to her in her profession.

'Learn from the sea, headmistress,' he had said, as they sat by the rocky shore of the island. 'If it can't take this boulder by storm, it will go round it, build up its forces elsewhere and then eventually submerge it.'

'It's had millions of years to do its work,' she had retorted. 'I reckon I've got ten years.' That had proved an over-estimate.

'Even so, you mustn't fight each engagement as if it were the last battle. If you lose over something you regard as important, withdraw, reform, come back at a later stage when they aren't expecting another onslaught.'

'Why did you appoint me? I hardly fit the mould of a famous girls' public school, do I? Not even a convert to orthodox education.'

'We had decided we needed to inject new life into the sluggish bloodstream and . . .'

'No, you. Why did you want me?'

'You woke me up, gave me a shock the moment you came into the room. I thought, if she can do that to me, she'll stir things up here. After all, that was what we were looking for, a challenge, a touch of abrasiveness.'

Spray blown on the breeze touched her cheek and, looking down, she saw that the sea had surrounded her little circle of sand and was already trickling between the rocks. The gap in the reef had been breached. She stood up, her knees shaking, and saw water running all around her. The breeze matted her hair with salt and stung the nape of her neck when she bent to take off her shoes. She tied the laces together and slung the shoes round the strap of her backpack, then she turned up the bottoms of her trousers and began to wade among the rocks; but although the water was still shallow there was a strong pull and several times she nearly fell. Everything was blurred and she could no longer see where to tread with safety. By the time she hauled herself on to the path, her feet were bleeding.

Two women, wading in high-heeled sandals, came past her as she limped along. One of them, nearly in tears, complained to the other, 'But it doesn't come in in a straight line.' Oh, the unfairness of life, Clarice thought. The old man with the pipe ignored her as she passed him. He had thought better of her.

She stuffed the paper napkin which had been wrapped around the sandwiches into one shoe and some tissues into the other to form a padding for her injured feet and made her way painfully to the car park. As she took lint and adhesive bandage from the first-aid box, she was grateful for these small wounds that with any luck would engage her mind on the return journey. No wonder penitents went barefoot. Much better than lying on a psychiatrist's couch regurgitating past errors.

But it wasn't wounds or past errors that kept her company on her journey. As she drove out of the long combe and saw above her a line of purple trailing a border of chequered green fields, she had again that sense of everything beginning to fall away from her of which she had complained when she was on the hill above the old mine with Alan; and, as the path climbed higher and higher, the more it seemed to her that this was irreversible, a condition which would not be altered by a change of landscape. The option of packing and going back to what had been home was not open to her. The path twisted and turned and the hunched shoulders lost their chequered green border.

The fear that had gripped her yesterday, when she read those words written in the diary, returned, chilling her to the bone. All around her now a dark moss green expanse stretched to the horizon. Colour was fading from the sky, which had become a pale egg-shell blue, infinitely cold. And suddenly, out of that desolation, emerged the figure of a woman walking, a long pole across her shoulders like a yoke with bundles attached to it. Clarice stopped the car and sat watching as the woman approached. There was no greeting, she had not expected one. As she went by, Clarice thought, 'The madwoman through the ages, tattered clothes and birds' nest hair; she's been around ever since exiles sat down to weep by the waters of Babylon. But the last time I saw her, she was younger, I'll swear to that.'

The sky was deep porcelain now and the moor a brown shadow.

Clarice said, 'All right. I'm making too much of her; she's a tramp, an old bag lady. But the other woman, she is real. In her world, which isn't my world — at least, I don't think it is, although I'm no longer very sure — but in whatever world she has her being, she is as real as I am.'

When at last she got back to the farm, Alan was waiting for her, looking rather like a loving dog, she thought, desperately anxious for the welfare of his meal ticket. Seeing him standing there in the yard, hunched in his anorak, she experienced a great need to cherish him, to hold on to him as never before. The warmth of their embrace surprised them both.

'I was beginning to get worried,' he said.

'I was well into worry. It was late and I tried to take a short cut and ended up above your blasted mine.'

'I expect you're tired,' he said speculatively.

'You want me to hear your lines?'

'It's just that I think this part is going to be too much for me.'

'You said that all through *Hamlet* and you got the Thames Valley award for best amateur performance.'

'I was fifteen years younger then,' he said, following her into the farm. 'And there are particular difficulties with playing a character who isn't involved in the action. If you're not careful the audience is going to wish old Gower would shuffle off for good and let the players get on with it.'

He came up to her bedroom with her and she heard him say his lines, listened to his anxieties about holding the attention of the audience, and made one or two tentative suggestions which he would not accept now but which would later become so much a part of his performance that he would be convinced he had thought of them himself. This seemed fair enough to her, used to being his subliminal voice.

'It's very comfortable here,' he said, looking around him. 'Much better than where I am. I've got Jimmy Howlett next door. His love-making's as laborious as the delivery of his lines. Different woman each night so far. I'm the constant factor. I haven't had a good night's sleep since I got here.'

'Do you want to move in here?'

He thought about this, weighing advantages. 'Bit isolated. The village is bad enough, if you can call it that, but there are several people from the other companies there as well as our lot.' He enjoyed the easy conviviality and the undemanding friendship of theatre people; a society in which one was accepted not so much for oneself as for the parts one played.

'Should we eat here?' he said. 'Then we could go to the pub afterwards.'

'I don't suppose that would be a problem. They give me enough food for two anyway.'

Later, as she looked at him across the table, the

lamplight making the thin face cadaverous, she thought that perhaps she hadn't tried enough to understand him. He wasn't Robert, but he was all she had and he was her one chance of getting a hold on a reality that threatened to slide away from her.

'Why are you so unsure of yourself?' she asked.

'I don't think I'm any more unsure of myself than any of the others. I'm confident once I get on stage.'

'I mean you. Not you playing Gower, or Hamlet, or one of Alan Ayckbourn's born losers.'

'I'm naturally melancholy.' He had long ago settled for melancholy, having discovered it was a subject few people were disposed to explore. 'It's a matter of one's type of person, I suppose.'

'What do you think your type of person is – apart from being melancholy?'

He helped himself to more potatoes, considering. 'Did I ever tell you about the questionnaire my wife and I got from the health farm?'

'No, you never did.'

'Well, you know she worked as a receptionist at a health farm? It seems some of the people had personality problems along with the weight problem. There was a questionnaire they were encouraged to fill in, rather like feeding your symptoms into a computer and having it come up with a diagnosis, only this was concerned with characteristics and responses to people and situations, rather than aches and pains. She insisted we both fill in one of these things. The idea was that it would tell you what type of person you were and this would make it easier for you to live with yourself, stop you straining to be someone else. It turned out that I belonged to a type that is two per cent of the population while she was run-of-the-mill forty per cent. She was furious – the way she talked you'd have thought I'd compiled the questionnaire rather than just filled it in to please her.'

'You mean she thought being two per cent was some sort of claim to superiority?'

'She said I always had to be different.'

'And did it make it easier for you to live with yourself, knowing there weren't many of you around?'

'I knew that anyway. They picked it up at school – although they didn't think it was a cause for con-gratulation.'

'You sound so reconciled to it, Alan. Doesn't it matter to you, being one on your own, more or less?'

He pursed his lips and frowned, a mime of thought she had long ago learnt to see through in the classroom. She persisted, 'Don't you feel you are always sending out signals no one is picking up?' Plainly, this was not how he felt; the idea that a signal might be emitted from his inner world was alarming. Whatever went on down there was not something on which he wished to receive an unsolicited report.

Clarice, however, was no longer concerned with Alan's reactions. 'I do it all the time – I send out signals to someone out there, someone who is of like mind, who strikes the same chords. A quiet listener sitting on the other side of the hearth, someone who understands the language of the heart. I never seem to meet them, not now, but they were there once. I'm sure they were there once, because I have such a sense of loss, as though a line of communication has been fouled.'

Involuntarily, Alan moved his hand, as though he would reach out to touch her hand, then, thinking better of it, turned the palm upward in a gesture of rueful regret for the inadequacy of life.

After a pause, Clarice said abruptly, 'Have you ever seen a ghost?'

'You know I haven't,' he said surprised. 'You must remember all the trouble I had with Nigel Winterton over those scenes with Hamlet's father's ghost, booming away in that sepulchral voice, and standing there swathed in mist. It was quite the wrong way to produce it.'

'What would have been the right way? Of understanding it, I mean, not of how to produce it?'

'An inner urge made visible, I suppose.'

'You mean Angela Wickham is really conjuring up a gardener she can leave to get on with it, without having to pay him?'

He brightened at the mention of Angela Wickham's ghostly gardener. 'No need to ensure he had had a tetanus injection, either. But what's your problem? Are you in need of some ghostly painter who will understand how to spring-clean your studio without actually moving one single object?'

'I'd have to find out first whether I believed in ghosts. Do you?'

'I don't fancy the idea. Life's cluttered enough as it is without finding spirits of another age using one's space. I think the way I feel about them is the way I know I shouldn't feel about foreigners – why don't they stay in their own country?'

'But what if they believe it is their country?'

'Mmh – bit beyond me, I'm afraid.'

Soon after this he returned to the pub, saying he could see that she was very tired. She stood in the porch for a little while looking into the night sky and thinking how odd it was that man, so fleeting a phenomenon, his lifespan so short, should have such a strong sense of possession.

The moon was up and it was a bright night, yet something cast an enormous shadow across the farmyard and the field beyond. As once before, she had the feeling of being overhung by walls much higher than those of the farmhouse.

Eight

'SHE SEES people,' Dame Ursula said. 'A woman, in particular.' She did not go any further than that because she could not bring herself to credit that the creature might have received a visitation.

The prioress, not herself notable for her humility, was merciless in putting down any pride in her nuns. She was well aware how Dame Ursula resented the thought that Joan Mosteyn might have received a visitation. She herself would have resented it had Dame Ursula been so favoured.

'Our Lady can appear in many guises,' she said severely. 'And it is noted that it is often to those whom we think foolish that she reveals herself.'

They both looked to where Joan Mosteyn sat sewing, the light shafting gently across her bowed head. She looked quite calm, although she was, in fact, bemoaning the unreasonableness of her husband.

There was great unrest in the country in 1463 and Martin Mosteyn was away from home much of the time on his lord's business. Joan was as ill-equipped to defend her hearth as the grape its vineyard. Certainly, she had not the wit to understand the interminable disputes that arose in her husband's absence, let alone settle them. There was little joy on his return.

'I told you this should not be allowed to continue,' he was shouting about some misdoing of one of the villeins. 'I wrote you instructions. Why did you not take the letter to the priest?'

'I've been trying to learn to read so that I can understand your instructions myself.' The steward was giving her instruction in that and much else, while neglecting more pressing duties.

'Trying to learn to read!' Their roles seemed to be reversed and Martin Mosteyn sounded for all the world like a shrewish wife, his voice shrill with frustration. 'You can't cook or sew or manage the servants, yet you waste time trying to learn to read.'

'I can't cook or sew,' she stamped a foot to emphasise each failing, 'or manage the house or read or write. And I'll not try to please you more.'

Martin was pale and quivering. He knew that he should have beaten her, but he was afraid to touch her; it was as though he had wakened a wild animal to a need to defend itself. Her rage died as quickly as it had flared up, but she made no apology and he did not have the courage to extort one. This the servants noted.

He had thought her a simple creature when he married her, but she had grown more unfathomable each time he returned home. Once her eyes had looked into his with such artless candour that he felt a shock run through his breast as though she had driven a stake deep into his soul; but now there was an inexplicable sadness in those eyes that he found the more disturbing. He punished her by refusing her need for clothing and cutting down the amount of food that was put before her; she was a slow eater, as she was slow in everything else, and if she lingered over a meal he made the servants take it away. But he did not beat her. When he made love to her he showed no tenderness. Once this had distressed her, but now she did not seem to care; when he hurt her, she moaned a little, but there was no reproach in the eyes that stared past him out of the window or into the shadows of the room, as though he were not there. Her indifference made him vicious, but even this she bore with stoicism; she was very strong physically. After he had been home only a short time, she began to complain of sickness and she told him that she was with child. This was a great relief to him. He became more generous, allowing her a few delicacies that she fancied and tolerating her indolent ways.

Joan was happy that summer and would often walk to the priory, where the nuns were kind to her and tried to teach her to sew. She would sit on a bench in the sun practising her stitches, full and content. The sun that shone day after day warmed her and hope surged within her so that her very heart seemed to expand. She had always felt herself to be trembling on the verge of some great happiness and now believed it would come to her with the birth of the baby, a creature especially designed to bring her delight. She was sure it was the steward's child.

'He was so beautiful,' she said. 'So beautiful. And my husband said that there must have been a gypsy in my family, for his people were never so swarthy.'

'This is the son she is talking about, fathered, it would seem, by her husband's steward,' Dame Ursula said, thin-lipped. 'She is forever in and out of the past.' This particular piece of the past she had no difficulty in crediting.

The prioress said, 'She is preparing to meet her end, as we all must, and she is reviewing her life, gathering up the threads.'

And a threadbare garment it would be when assembled, Dame Ursula thought.

Nine

EDWARD TRESHAM had come across an old history of the moor. It was not a work of scholarship, being more concerned with folklore and anecdote, but he had read it in the hope that it might contain details of the building of Foxlow Priory, about which so little seemed to be known. It became plain as he read, however, that the author knew rather less than Edward himself. He put the book aside and immediately the anxieties he had been trying to keep at bay took possession of his mind.

The lamp he had lit flickered in a draught; he had placed it on the window-sill so that Rhoda would see it when she came into the yard. Daylight was only just beginning to die and there was really no need of the lamp, but it gave him comfort. In the room below he could hear Eleanor, Rhoda's cousin, admonishing the children. When he had gone downstairs to seek his wife ten minutes ago, she had told him that Rhoda had gone for a walk, tossing the remark over her shoulder as though it were of no consequence, while she busied herself with sorting linen.

'I would rather Rhoda didn't do this,' he had said, but she had only shrugged and replied, 'She'll come to no harm. Harold's up there, he'll keep an eye on her.'

'Your husband can hardly survey the whole moor.'

'And 'tis fine and dry and the air will do her good.' A

woman incapable of attending to more than one thing at a time, Edward thought, as he left her folding sheets.

He regretted the decision to come here, but Rhoda had been ill and longed for the place, and in his weakness he had humoured her. The building, which until the beginning of the century had been an inn, was possessed of a set of rooms which, although now normally occupied by the farmer and his wife, could on occasions be set aside for guests. He could have wished their lodging a little less comfortable; she might then have been subjected to the full rigours and crudity of farm life and severed her romantic attachment to it.

He heard her footsteps in the yard and stood looking down while their daughter ran out to greet her mother, a lively, dancing creature of ten years, who usually lightened his heart. Today, when he felt himself separated from them in sympathy and understanding, the sight of these two, his dearest possessions, wrenched at his heart.

'Veronica so enjoys being with the other children, I have said she may stay down there for another half-hour,' Rhoda said apologetically when she entered the room. Then, seeing his drawn face, she came and laid a hand on his arm. 'My dear, there was no need to worry. See how well wrapped I am.'

'But you should not go out alone on the moor.'

'I only walked as far as the shepherd's hut.'

'The place is not good for you,' he said as he helped her out of her cloak, noticing with joy and fear how she emerged from the brown cloth like a butterfly from its chrysalis. 'I know it draws you, but there is something morbid in this strange fascination.'

She looked up at him, smiling, hoping to ease him out of this unhappy mood. 'It is not a fascination, Edward. This is the place where I grew up and it is home to me.' She smoothed the sleeves of her gown with little nervous gestures and he noticed how fine and fragile were her wrists.

'Home is in London,' he reproved her. 'You can't know how much you wound me when you say these things.'

'I meant only that it is familiar and friendly,' she answered lightly, trying to keep the conversation from becoming too serious.

'Friendly, that!' He thrust his arm towards the window in an uncharacteristically dramatic gesture.

She fetched the lamp from the window-sill, pausing for a moment to look at the hills, now rapidly darkening as the light failed. 'It is friendly because it is familiar.' Nevertheless, she turned away and brought the lamp to the table. 'Just as you find your first sight of Highgate Hill welcomes you when we return, so, as the path climbs up from the river, I can smell the air and . . . '

'The air here is bad for you.'

She sat by the fire, which he had neglected in his distress. 'But it is as fresh at the end of the day as it is in the morning. You cannot say that of the London air.' She picked up the poker. 'I don't know what has happened here, Edward; you are usually so . . . '

'The London air is not so harsh as this.' He took the poker from her and went down on one knee to consider where to place it to the best effect.

'And I like the great distances here. In London everything crowds in so.'

He looked into her face. 'You have no idea what a

misery it is to me to know you are so unhappy in your home.'

She leant forward and put her hands on his shoulders, returning look for look. 'Edward, that is hardly fair. When have I ever complained or said that I am unhappy? All I ask is that you should allow me to be happy here, too, on this holiday to which you have so generously consented. How can you possibly object to my being happy in two places?'

He turned away and set his mind to the fire and she thought this would be an end to it. Later, however, when their daughter was in bed, and Millie had brought them tea, he said, 'But you must admit, my dear, there is so much pleasure in London that we both share, the walks in the park, the opportunity to hear music, to visit the exhibitions . . . '

'Yes, all these are great pleasures,' she assented, but averted her face and looked into the fire.

'A much greater pleasure,' he persisted, 'you must surely admit, than any offered here. If you are honest, you will admit there is no comparison.'

She said to the fire, 'Pleasure, yes; perhaps that is so.'

He knew she was thinking of something beyond pleasure that she found walking out there on the moor. Even now, as she thought about it, she had withdrawn from him into a world he could not share. He needed to possess her soul and to establish a secure place in her mind even more than he needed her body. He could never be at ease unless he knew what was going on inside all the people who mattered to him. At such moments as this, he was like an animal who cannot know when its mistress leaves it whether she has gone for an hour or for ever. His despair was absolute. No assurances, no promises, could reach him at such times. Once she moved outside the range of his own thoughts and pursuits she was lost to him. He could not trust her to be herself and still love him.

He said, desperate to recall her, 'When you make so little of the things that matter to me, you make little of me, too. Do you realise that?'

She turned to him in distress. 'But I don't make little of the things that matter to you, Edward. Only now you spoke of the love of music we share, of our walks in the park to which I look forward each day.'

'You spoke of them as pleasure.'

'I think it was you who did that, Edward. I but followed you.'

'But with such contempt. You have a contempt for the pleasures of my mind.'

'Never, Edward! Oh, believe me, my dear, I have the greatest respect for your mind.' She clasped her hands together in a gesture that was both eager and supplicating. 'I see you as a good householder, making room for the proper furniture with which you can live so that your mind becomes a repository of treasures.' She saw that her words were not reaching him, so icy was his despair. 'It is only that we respond in different ways that makes this difficulty between us. If I could but make you understand!' She turned her head to one side and looked at the shadows gathering beyond the circle of light shed by the lamp; when she spoke it seemed as if she was addressing some unseen person. This was her only way of confiding her deeper thoughts.

'You are so cultured, Edward, and you have such a depth of knowledge, that you must make allowance for my lack. I am incapable of the kind of appreciation that you are able to give to a work of art. But for me, sometimes, very rarely, there is a moment of recognition, the sharing of an experience – my own experience, clarified, beatified, even. It is like coming to a cave in a wild, unpopulated place and finding a painting, or a tool even, that tells me someone has been there before me – it's not the disappointment of the explorer who wants to venture where no human has been, for whom the importance is to be the first, but the tremendous reassurance that in the remotest place humanity has existed and left this message from thousands of years ago. That Greek sculpture of the shepherd boy, that you thought rudimentary – archaic, I think you told me – affected me in that way, direct, without intermediary.'

He looked at her, scarcely able to believe that she could refer to that time in Greece when he had first realised the gulf between them, had stood on its giddying brink.

She was feeling her way towards something that was very difficult for her, but she went on, wanting to make a gift to him, however imperfectly articulated. 'Perhaps because I haven't your learning, experiences like that don't usually come to me in art galleries or museums; it is places that seem to confront me in that way.' She paused to reflect on this, then nodded. 'Yes, confront. The moor confronts me.'

His face was bloodless, nostrils pinched, the lips dry and puckered; when he was like this he seemed withered to the bone. After a time, perhaps no more than a matter of seconds although to him it seemed like minutes, she turned towards him. 'Edward?'

He roused himself. 'What nonsense you have been talking, my dear. I see that we must not discuss, it tires your brain.' He got up and went to the window to draw the curtains. When he turned she had picked up a book that she had earlier laid on the stool by the fire. There were bright spots of colour on her cheeks that he did not much like, but her face seemed composed, even haughty. There was a point beyond which she would not be driven in her efforts to comfort him. At such times, his fears for her health became disquiet about the woman herself.

'I thought we might make an excursion tomorrow,' he said. 'A change of scene would be pleasant and I recall when we were last here there was a delightful village in a wooded valley with a stream running through it. The colour of the trees should be superb now.'

She said, without looking up, 'Yes, that would be agreeable.'

'That is, if you would enjoy it?'

'As you say, the trees will be particularly fine.'

'I hope you are not annoyed, my dear?'

'No, I am not annoyed, Edward.'

She turned a page.

'I expect Veronica would greatly like to have time with us. She has been very patient with the children, but she is, after all, older and needs more mature companions.'

'I am sure she would like it.'

'Indeed, she must be prepared for a more mature environment since she is to go to this school that you are convinced will be of such benefit to her.'

She looked up from the book, surprised by this un-expected gift, as he had meant her to be. 'That is very generous of you, Edward.'

'I only want what is good for you, my dear.'

'It will be good for her, Edward, I know it will.'

He bowed his head; he had made his sacrifice and would not go back on his promise, but he was not prepared to accept that good might come of it for Veronica. He saw it only as a means of keeping one of his treasures in his safe-keeping. Their daughter, by the nature of things, he would probably lose anyway, and had been preparing himself for that sorrow. But he could not resist saying, 'So long as you can bear her loss; I am afraid that is something you may not have taken into account.'

'It is a day school, Edward. We shall not lose her.'

'Do you realise the subjects she will be studying? She will cease to be the unaffected, spontaneous girl who is such a delight to us.'

'That would go along with her girlhood, anyway; and she will become an interesting woman in whose learning we shall delight.'

'Let us hope so.' He entertained no such hope himself.

Out in the yard the dogs were barking, their quick ears picking up the sound of horse's hooves while the rider was still some little distance from the farm. Voices sounded below and soon they heard the farmer greeting the newcomer. Edward said, 'Surely that is the vicar again? I think you should stay here until I find out what tidings he brings.' But she followed him out of the room.

It was dark outside now and the rider filled the threshold. Perhaps they saw him framed there for no more than a matter of seconds, but for that time he seemed to hold the night at bay. Then he stepped into the house, a tired man but with some energy still at his command. As he shouldered off his cloak, Jory told them, 'The little maid is not with the sister. She said Jarvis hadn't been near her for a twelvemonth.'

Harold said heavily, 'Then we'll start a search at first light.'

Eleanor put her hand to her face and moaned, rocking to and fro, 'Oh, dear Lord, dear Lord!'

Jory said, 'The villagers are out already.'

'And Jarvis?' Harold was to the point, irritated by his wife's wailing.

'Gone, no one knows where. For his own safety, it would be better were he to be taken into custody.'

'His own safety!' Edward, whose peace was greatly disturbed by this, could scarcely believe what he had heard. 'It would be better were he to be hanged here and now.'

Jory turned, subjecting Edward to a brief, dispassionate appraisal. 'For what would you hang him? The child has yet to be found.'

'But will be soon enough. This is a rough land, I would have thought summary justice still prevailed.'

Although Jory did not speak slowly, it was noticeable that he never allowed himself to be rushed; he made space for words and this made his listeners take note of him. 'I have read enough in the old records at the church and in the parsonage to make any man sicken of summary justice. People were burnt as witches not far from here for no worse crime than that among the sick whom they tended a few happened to die.'

'But this man, Jarvis . . . '

'It's Jarvis's child we have to find.'

'And you expect to find her alive?'

Again that thoughtful appraisal, after which he decided no answer to be necessary.

Eleanor moaned, 'Oh, I should have done more. Leastways, I should have done less complaining that he owed rent.'

The farmer said angrily, 'Let's have no more o' that nonsense.'

'But it's been on my mind, Harold. He's such a lying, thriftless creature and I got so angry with 'm.'

'I want to hear no more o' that. Now get into the kitchen and find out what Millie's about. Mr Jory here needs food after his journey.'

She went away crying into the kitchen and the farmer said to Jory, 'Come in here, where we can talk without this weeping and wailing.'

Edward turned to Rhoda, who was standing half-way down the stairs. She was as still as people are in that moment when they hold an indrawn breath; in the lamplight her dress shimmered, it was the only thing about her that appeared to have motion. 'Now you realise it,' he said triumphantly. 'Evil! That's what confronts you out on the moor. Evil!'

Her eyes looked over his shoulder at the half-open door into the parlour, where firelight reflected the shadow of one man on the wall.

Ten

'OH, DEAR lady, you look so beautiful standing there. I see such sorrow in your eyes that I am sure you see me and that you have come to help me. I loved my children, I wasn't a good mother, but I loved them . . .'

'Joan, what happened to your children?' Dame Priscilla asked gently.

'Leave her,' Dame Ursula said. 'At least she becomes quieter when she talks to Our Lady.'

'But it may help her.'

'Are you suggesting we may help, rather than Our Lady?'

'It was after the Battle of Tewkesbury, dear Lady,' Joan said, addressing her reply to the space where she usually seemed to locate the lady, whom she persisted in describing as wearing a shimmering lavender gown, although this was not one of the accepted attributes of the Virgin. 'I can't recall quite when that was.'

'It was in 1471,' Dame Ursula said, tricked into taking part in this discussion by a desire to make a show of her knowledge of events some fifteen years past. 'Queen Margaret was taken prisoner and her son killed.'

'Your children . . . ' Dame Priscilla prompted Joan, not minded to take a history lesson from Dame Ursula.

'I had two children; the boy by the steward and a girl

by my husband. A mismatched pair who quarrelled much . . .'

Martin had told her she was a bad mother, never instructing or beating the children. She was not good at anything women were supposed to be good at: seeing to the running of the household, sewing, rearing children. She had no trouble in loving the children. The boy, who was now eight, grew daily more like the steward, long since departed. Each time she looked at that dark head, the hair curling crisply at the nape of the neck, she trembled with longing and could hardly conceal the agitation of her limbs from her husband.

She did not attempt to control the two children and when her husband was away from home they rampaged, doing as they wished. She enjoyed, and even encouraged, their high spirits; their appetite for mischief satisfied something in herself. But when Martin came home they were a sore trial to her and in an attempt to gain control she would shout abuse and throw anything that came to hand. Once, it was a lighted brand that scarred her son's lovely face. She hadn't meant any harm, she had never meant any harm in all her life. But the servants whispered among themselves.

News came that spring of a battle near Tewkesbury. A troupe of players brought tales of it, but people treated them much as they did the scenes the players performed and, indeed, in the telling of it it was difficult to distinguish fact from fantasy.

Martin Mosteyn had never been in a battle and had not intended to be in this one, only the fighting had overflowed into the lane down which he was riding on his way to deliver a message to his lord's brother. He had been clobbered about the head and had lain for a long time in a ditch. What happened after that he had been unable to recall very clearly, nor did he know how he came by the charger which carried him home, slumped more dead than alive in the saddle.

Joan sent for the nuns' priest, who was reputed to know about medicine, as he knew about most things. The priest did not, in fact, know very much, but he could recognise a dying man when he saw one.

'He has a fever,' he told Joan.

'But he has wounds, too. Do you think my lord might send his physician if he knew? Martin has been dutiful in his service.'

The priest doubted if his lordship would wish to be concerned with a humble squire at this time, but to satisfy her he said he would see what could be done. He went away and Joan was so occupied in tending Martin that she had no time to lose hope as the hours drained away.

At some stage of his journey, Martin Mosteyn had begun to think of his wife as she was when he first saw her. 'Full and golden, full and golden as the harvest moon,' he whispered as she bent over him. He would have no one else beside him, which suited the servants, who could not bear the stink of him. When she moved away from the bed, he shrieked and clutched at her gown. It was no use trying to reason with him, his mind twitched and jerked as much as his body. Joan dressed his wounds and bathed his face as best she could. All the love and longing he had never been able to express towards her now seemed to overflow; he repeated her name over and over again and babbled endearments.

There was an old woman in the village who could work remarkable cures and she came to the house to tell Joan what she should do, but her remedies seemed to Joan to be very painful and she said, 'He is in such pain already, it would not seem kind to make him suffer more.'

The servants were shocked that she would not do as the old woman told her. They knew of her seduction by the steward and imagined that she planned to have him back and make him master of the manor.

When she was asked if she wished to send for the priest she said, 'Later, later,' because Martin claimed all her attention and she had no time to think about fetching the priest. She had no more forethought as to dying than to living and imagined the most important task she had to perform was to remain with Martin, to comfort him and ease his pain. This she did tirelessly; it seemed to come naturally to her, just as making love had come naturally, and little else besides.

In the early morning, just before daybreak, he became calmer and the fever seemed to leave him; he lay quiet, his face thin, the nose like the beak of a bird. He looked at her wonderingly and she put her hands over his, confident that a miracle had been worked and that all would be well. Outside, a blackbird perched on the chimney was singing. She bent forward, regardless of the foulness of his being, and rested her cheek against his; when she moved away, his eyes had turned up.

He had died without being shriven. A thrill of horror ran through the household at the presence of evil.

The priest when he came was revolted by her brute stupidity; but he had smelt enough burnt flesh in his time and considered it worth some effort to save her from her folly.

'You would be advised to leave here. Can you not go to one of your sisters?'

'But the manor belongs to my son now. And in any case, I could not go to my sisters. They would have me live as they do, and that I should not like.'

The day after her husband was buried, she walked in the hills, gazing in wonder at the land of which Martin had had the care. She felt very grateful to her husband and proud of him. The thought that someone else must now look to the care of the land did not immediately occur to her. She was a naturally hopeful person and thought that life would be easier in future.

In the fields there were children who should have been working, but were laughing and playing. As she came towards them, they ran away; she called after them to reassure them, but they ran all the faster. One of them had a fever that night.

'Oh, dear Lady, I loved the children . . . '

Eleven

WHILE HER husband was out riding Rhoda took the opportunity to write her diary.

I see them both so clearly and they see me, but whether they see each other, I do not know.

The years have composed the face of the older one, although the eyes are searching still. But the other one vibrates with the expectations of youth and I wonder if she is one of those who never become reconciled to disappointment. Certainly, she seems to know little of discipline. Sometimes she sings, and then her voice echoes as it would not in this house and I think she is singing in the priory, from the stones of which this house was built. But the other one . . . I am becoming more than ever convinced that she lives in a world of which we have no knowledge.

Nothing like this has ever happened to me before. Edward would say that it is because of this place, or it is the state of my mind. But I do not think either of these explanations is the right one. I begin to get some inkling of the truth and, if I am right, then I know that I must not turn away from the strange visitors who share these moments with me.

We do not speak, but their eyes carry a message and I begin to understand what that message is. Do they see that same message in my eyes, I wonder?

Twelve

'Is there anyone out there?' asked Pericles.

'I'm sorry,' Clarice said. 'I've lost the place.'

'So have I, dear.'

'You do realise,' the director said at the end of the morning rehearsal, 'that we only have two more days before we go up?'

A dispirited silence acknowledged their awareness.

'There's no more I can say, is there? I've done all I possibly can. It's up to you whether you want to put on a good show or not.'

They bowed their heads and avoided eye contact. This, they knew from previous experience, was the calm indifference that follows the storm. Or, as Alan put it to Clarice as they ate their packed lunch up on the moor, 'The moment when the gods depart from the earth leaving the mortals to wallow in their own mire.'

'It was rather awful,' she said.

'A shipwreck, indeed.'

She watched a bird poised still above a thicket. 'Is that a buzzard?'

'A kestrel. You can't possibly think it's a buzzard – however many times do I have to tell you?'

'Until seventy times seven, it would seem.'

She looked down into the valley below where water

rushed dark green, silvered with foam.

'Do you ever dream of your daughter?' she asked Alan.

'Mmh. Usually just before she gets in touch to grumble about her mother.'

'I dreamt last night. I can't get it out of my mind.'

He looked at her, but said nothing, waiting to see whether she wanted to go on. It was one of the things she prized in him, that he could listen to her silences. Eventually, she did go on.

'I dreamt of a girl, a light, dancing creature – she wasn't Teresa Davies and yet she was her.'

'Often the way in dreams.'

'Yes, I sometimes think they use the same technique as the short story writer, getting the maximum mileage out of each image. There are people within people. This girl, who wasn't Teresa and yet so surely was her, was more rounded physically, plump in fact, with dimpled cheeks and elbows. A Victorian miss. She was talking to her father about a cook. I could recall the dialogue when I woke up.

'He said, "I think Mrs Possett is preparing to leave us."

'She replied, "Oh, I must go and talk to her."

' "Might it not be better were she to go?"

' "No, Father, we should find it very difficult to obtain anyone so satisfactory as Mrs Possett."

' "What are we coming to if we have to regard Mrs Possett as satisfactory? When I was young we had a succession of admirable cooks."

' "No, Father, the very fact of their being a succession proves they were not admirable. You only think Mrs Possett is worse because you observe her more clearly now that it is you and not Mama who must deal with her while I am at school."

'I think there was a bit more, but the traces have faded.'

Alan said, 'It was rather good – not unlike Goldsmith, would you say, except the bit about being at school?'

She looked down at the water swelling as the river widened out beyond a little bridge until one felt it must free a passage on to the greensward. She said in a low voice, 'The mother wasn't there. Why was that?'

'Probably died in childbirth,' Alan suggested, only mildly interested. 'So many women did at that time.'

'Not this one.'

'You knew that in the dream?'

'Not in the dream – at least, not in that dream.' She looked at him speculatively, needing his help but not sure how much she could tell him without asking for an involvement he was unable to offer. At the moment he seemed more interested in a fastidious examination of his sandwich than in what she was saying. 'I was so disturbed, isn't it silly?'

'It doesn't sound disturbing; pleasantly domestic, in fact, told in the daylight.'

The qualification encouraged her. 'It was the school that did it. It set up echoes in my mind. Your name was put down for public school while you were in the womb and you took education as a matter of course, a process that had to be gone through. For me, and for the girl in my dream, it was a gift that would enable us to comprehend our world and move about in it with confidence.' She pushed the short curls back from her forehead as though the gesture might clear cobwebs from the mind. 'But there's no magic prescription, is there? No Golden Road – we each have our own Samarkand. If the girl in my dream is who I think she is, she had seven children and it was one of her *daughters* who truly seized the gift.'

'Is this your headmistress, Miss Wilcox?'

'Yes. You know how I feel about her. I must have told you often enough. I was so grateful that I thought I must go into education myself. I didn't understand that what she really handed to me was space to find my own way. It was left to Teresa to restore that space to me.'

'At some cost.'

'There's always a cost, isn't there?'

Alan, not entirely easy with this notion, looked up at the sky as though seeking some signal, perhaps a threat even, that might make a move advisable. Failing to find any such portent, he said reluctantly, 'It brought it all back, I suppose?'

'It was so mixed up, so many feelings; I couldn't identify them all as mine even, some belonged to the dream people, you know the way it can happen. Sometimes you don't know who's doing the dreaming – it's as if you were outside watching someone else's dream. But I *was* in it, not just a spectator, because I woke up crying, "Teresa, don't go away!" It's a good thing there's no one in the room next to mine.'

Alan turned back the corner of a sandwich suspiciously; he had noted that the farm seemed to be more generous with meat than the pub on which he was dependent. 'Do you dream of her often?'

'Not now. She hovers around sometimes indirectly. But

it's years since I've seen her so vividly. And even then, the face wasn't hers.'

They finished their lunch in silence, each absorbed in private thoughts. As she collected the rubbish, Clarice said, 'She was Marina in the school production of *Pericles* – a glowing performance, half inspiration, half the incandescence of youth. There are other scenes in *Pericles* that are darker and the players in those scenes were there, too, waiting in the wings of my dream.'

'Let it lie,' Alan advised. 'If it's significant, I expect there'll be a sequel.'

Clarice said, 'Yes, I'm afraid there will.'

There was a rehearsal in the evening and by now there wasn't time to walk down to the village below. 'I told you we should have brought beer with us,' she said as they turned in the direction of the farm some four miles away.

'I should only go to sleep. We can't afford another bad rehearsal.'

As they walked the sun changed the scene more effectively than any theatre lighting expert. At one moment there were soft bands of mother of pearl across a cool blue sky and all was quiet and unemphatic. Then it grew dark and the moor became an undifferentiated dun mass. A brief reappearance of the sun brightened the dark hills and bobbled the sky with orange and eau de Nil. Soon the colours changed more rapidly; the moor was streaked with brown and grey while on a near slope a shaft of sun cast a vivid lime-green spotlight, creating an arena surrounded by an already dark amphitheatre.

When they had meekly assembled, all on time, in the theatre, the director said, 'We'll take the scene with

Antiochus and his daughter – and try to get the riddle right this time, Pericles; it does, after all, contain the nature of this relationship.'

'My mother never let me read about such things,' Pericles murmured coyly. The director pretended not to hear.

The king and his daughter took up their positions. On the edges of the action the followers stood round. When the director had said he would use masks for the followers one of them had protested that he felt he should be expressing something.

'What do you want to express?'

'I don't quite know . . . '

'The masks do know.'

And watching the strange archaic faces with the gashed mouths and burnt-out eyes, Clarice thought the director had been right.

The lights in the theatre dimmed, leaving only a circle of light encompassing the players. Gower spoke, and the masked faces watched as the human drama unfolded.

Thirteen

I

THE DOOR swung slowly on its hinge. There was a rustling in a pile of sacking in the corner and something, a rat perhaps, scuttled across the floor. Joan stood at the door, but did not go any further. The light was fading now, but she did not need more light to see that the kitchen was empty of human occupants. She looked over her shoulder back towards the gallery. Somewhere up there a window, left half-open, rattled as a gust of wind blew down the stairs. She took a few paces into the hall, put one foot on the stairs and paused, her hand on the rail, looking up into the gallery. She went up the first two steps; they creaked, she had never noticed before how wood creaked and cracked at night. Half-way up the stairs, she sat down, facing the hall. Her eyes moved warily from side to side, no longer trying to discover a presence in the house but exploring her fears.

They had all gone. She had been down to one of the villeins' cottages to see the seamstress; it was only a short distance and it had taken her little more than three-quarters of an hour, but in that time the house had emptied. Even the children were gone.

The servants had grown more insolent over the

months since Martin Mosteyn died, and behind their insolence lay something else, an inexplicable fear. Joan told herself she should be glad they were gone. But the children . . .

She got to her feet and edged up the stairs, keeping close to the wall; she came to the window in the gallery and, standing to one side, looked out. The fields came close to the house on this side and often at this hour she had seen hares leaping; now, nothing moved. She looked in the direction of the wooded valley and then the other way, towards the village. The breeze had momentarily died down and even the long spear-headed grass was still.

She said, 'So that's all right, then,' and walked along the gallery, her arms crossed, fingers gripping the flesh above each elbow. She set her feet down carefully, anxious not to disturb this strange peace. She went into her chamber and sat on the window-sill. She could see the track that led to the village. Near at hand were the outhouses. A horse moved in the stables; the horses were restless tonight. Perhaps they had not been fed?

'I will get my own supper,' she said. 'Now, while it is quiet.' But she stayed at the window, looking at the track that led to the village.

An owl flew out from one of the barns on silent wings. She clapped her hands over her mouth, thinking it an ill omen, and waited, fearful lest her own movement should have stirred something out there, beyond the outhouses. It was nearly dark now, she could no longer see the track and the line of the barns was beginning to merge into the blackness of the fields.

'I hope they don't come back drunk,' she said. 'I'd as

97

soon they didn't come back if they are drunk, only I must find where they have taken the children.'

She went along the gallery and stood on the threshold of the small chamber where the children and the old nurse slept. The room was empty, as though no one had ever been there. Suddenly, she flung herself down, pulling at the bedding, feeling among the rushes strewn on the floor; while she did this she howled like a dog baying at the moon. Then, as suddenly, she stopped, terrified by her own activity. Her heart thumped and she put her hand to her breast to quiet it. Her eyes had lost their half-dreaming expression and were sharp as those of an animal. She crossed the floor, hunched low, and peered out of the slit window. Things had changed in the short time since she last looked out. Now the darkness was pierced by tiny points of light that had sprung up well beyond the outhouses and crissed and crossed and then seemed all to wheel round in a merry dance of flame and then to stretch into a line. The line began to thread its way along the track from the village. She ran into the gallery and leant out of the window; a noise no louder than the murmur of bees on a summer day came to her ears. She crouched, staring, her eyes wide, her mouth hanging open foolishly. The points of light lengthened and grew brighter. In the stable, the horses began to thrash about. She jerked up and, gathering her skirts around her thighs, ran down the stairs, her feet sending up thudding echoes in the empty house. She had bolted the outer door to the yard and now her frenzied fingers failed to draw the bolt. Instead of persisting, she abandoned the effort and ran to one of the hall windows. Ruddy light streamed upward and she could see, following the column of flame, the dark outline of wildly gyrating figures. Crimson light reflected on the window-pane.

She ran to the outer door and this time managed to draw back the bolt. Which way to run? She had always felt free in the fields, but they led on to heathland, open country. She needed to be on the far side of the house where she could run downhill into the shelter of the wooded valley. She crouched, panting, unable to think what to do, her eyes staring in fascination at the flames that leapt up where bracken was already ablaze. There had been no rain for a long time and the ground was tinder dry. Something moved round the side of the house and a figure, bent low, scurried across the yard. She opened her mouth to scream, but had no breath for that. A body crashed down beside her, fingers grasped her wrist. She recognised him by the sour smell of his breath: it was the priest.

'Save me! Save me, good sir!' She clutched at his arm.

He began to drag her back towards the house. They could smell burning tar now. The roar of voices seemed rent from some great beast maddened by the scent of blood.

'Your husband's clothes,' he said. 'There must be something you can wear.'

'I must get away,' she screamed. 'I must, I must . . . '

'You won't get away by running.' He had pushed open the outer door and now he paused and turned her round. 'Look!'

The torches were coming from all directions, the night was ablaze and close at hand two great, three-pronged torches tilted towards one of the outhouses.

'Listen!' he commanded. 'When the barns are well ablaze, we will join the throng.' He dragged her across the threshold of the house. 'Take off your gown. I will make some kind of dummy to prop at this window. It will divert them long enough for our purpose.'

But she was incapable with terror. He tore the gown from her and he it was who opened first one chest, then another, finding a pair of breeches here, a shirt there. There was dust a-plenty to darken her face. Momentarily emboldened by the strange garb the child in her awoke; she switched her hair up on top of her head and pulled an old woollen sock over it, low down on her forehead. The excitement of being someone else outweighed her fear.

The yard was brighter than day now and the barns were alight. He stuffed a bundle of clothing into Joan's discarded gown and propped it close to the window, standing well back himself while Joan crouched on the ground. They went down the stairs and had reached the hall when there was a splintering of wood and a jet of flame gushed forth. It was too late to get out of the house. As men rushed into the hall the priest pushed Joan into the little room where her husband's steward had kept his accounts. Voices were screaming, 'Burn the witch! Burn the witch!' Someone threw a flaming torch through the door of the room in which they crouched and ran on. The priest bent and picked up the torch, then he caught Joan by the arm and forced her into the hall. They ran forward shouting, 'Burn the witch!' The priest thrust the torch into the face of a man who came too close. He reeled back, lost his footing and dropped his torch along with his life. Joan bent down and picked it up. The man's hair was already on fire. They ran on. Joan cried, 'Burn the witch!' It gave her courage and she shouted louder, 'Burn the witch!' Then she began to scream without ceasing, 'Burn the witch, burn the witch, burn the witch!' She lost all sense of herself, madness took possession of her and she leapt exultant in the flames. The stairs were alight and there were men trapped above. A window shattered as someone jumped. A man rushed past Joan and the priest screaming, his clothing ablaze. The priest dragged Joan towards the stone-flagged kitchen where the flames had not yet gained a hold. She was screaming wildly, 'Burn the witch!'

He had to wrest the torch from her. He threw it back into the doorway and his own after it. The fire was raging everywhere now, the barns were well alight, animals thrashing and shrieking. Men ran from the furnace, blind with panic, not knowing which way to go to escape. Outside Joan, too, wanted to run. Flames leapt high into the night sky, but she wanted to dash through them in the direction of the fields. The priest stayed her. The wind was stronger. He waited to see in which direction it was blowing.

'This way.' He pulled her along the side of the house. Flames reached out to them as they ran; ahead, the trees were alight and streamers of flame danced into the air and ran along the ground. It seemed at first there was no way out. But the priest, who had no mind to be martyred in his efforts to save this foolish creature, kept his wits about him. The flames were rolling east. Their only chance lay on the far side of the blazing house. He dragged Joan with him. No one paid heed to them. Had she been recognised it would no longer have mattered to the frantic people around them.

In the direction of the wood there was an area of darkness and they ran towards it. The flames roared and crackled, burning the soles of their feet. They were blinded by smoke and their lungs were bursting; but they stumbled on, driven by fear of the fire that gained hold rapidly as though the parched soil rushed forward to meet it.

The wood and the valley lay beneath them. Once they reached the shelter of the trees they lay down, panting, to recover breath; but soon they had to haul themselves up as flame spiralled around them. It was no longer possible to tell which way the fire was going. They began to lose their senses and even the priest staggered sometimes dazedly towards the fiery torch trees. In the undergrowth, animals ran; the wood was alive and moving. The burning trees roared as though welcoming their destroyer with a hymn of praise. Joan and the priest went with the animals. At last, when it seemed there was a ring of flame closing in on them, they came to the bank of a stream. There was no water there now, but the bank was very steep and the bed of the stream was wide; this clearing might afford some shelter, though it was doubtful whether it would be enough to hold back the flames. If it wasn't, they must die. Death seemed more welcome now than further effort. Joan was almost unconscious as she half-rolled, half-fell into the bed of the stream – a refuge that they shared with many terrified live animals and not a few dead ones, some of which had died of thirst and whose bodies were in varying stages of decay.

Above them, the flames roared and trees came down like flaming towers; once a trunk fell across the stream making a bridge of fire. The heat became intense and it seemed this alone would kill them for it was impossible to breathe in this furnace, although they lay with their faces pressed against the stones so that the air would not sear their lungs. And then there came a roar louder than anything they had heard and they looked up fearfully, expecting the whole wood to come down on top of them. Eerie light flickered above the flames and twisted away. Joan croaked, 'Sweet Jesus, forgive me!' thinking herself already dead, but the priest gasped, 'Lightning.' As though in answer to his words, the rain came down, blinding, torrential.

The rain lasted for many hours and when it dwindled to spasmodic pattering, they crawled up the bank. Around them the wood steamed and stank. Joan sat shivering on a charred stump. As she tried to dry herself it occurred to her that she could not go back for a change of clothing.

'I can never go back,' she said, speaking aloud at the wonder of it.

II

Rhoda Tresham experienced the dreaded heat of fever. It did not, fortunately, cause her body to shake; the effect was in her mind, which was ablaze with light. In the past such experiences had led inevitably to a crippling headache. She waited in dread, not daring to move. Mercifully, the headache did not come, but the sense of violent heat persisted. As she lay still beside Edward, praying she might not wake him, she feared that in the morning she would find herself to have been blinded by the intensity of light behind her eyeballs. Many times during her marriage she had lain imposing stillness on her body for fear of arousing Edward, whose anxiety was a heavier burden than her illnesses. This often led to a bout of sickness. She prayed she might not be sick tonight. Her mouth was so dry she could scarcely swallow, but she dared not reach out for the water container that stood on the little cabinet beside the bed. She sometimes wondered whether her indispositions might not have passed more quickly had she not been driven to conceal them.

When at last morning came, she turned away from its enquiring light and pretended to sleep, fearing the effect her ravaged face must have on her husband. It was a surprise when, after he had gone downstairs, she opened her eyes and found the room presented to her, neat and orderly, in sharp focus. The face that looked back at her from the mirror showed no sign of the night's searing; in fact, if anything, there was less colour in her cheeks than usual. The violet eyes were clear, though underlined with shadow; this she could pass off, could make use of even by insisting on the outing she had planned yesterday in response to Edward's suggestion of an expedition to the town where he wished to visit a museum recently opened.

'While you are at the museum,' she had said, 'I would like to visit the school of which Mr Jory is so proud. I think it only polite that we should show an interest.'

The Reverend Jory was as convinced of the importance of education as was Rhoda – 'only my interest is in the needs of the poor who have no opportunity to better themselves,' he had said; a remark that had shocked Edward, who feared the effects of education on the poor for the very reason that it might encourage them to better themselves.

Rhoda poured water into the glass and drank. Her throat was still parched and it took another glass to slake her thirst. This apart, she felt ready for the day, if a little shaky mentally.

At breakfast, Edward made his disapproval of 'this venture of Jory's' apparent.

'The venture is a joint one,' Rhoda pointed out, 'since the money was provided by Sir James Meredith whom you have always regarded as a great benefactor of this area and whose politics you so admire. And it is not so far to West Bentham as the journey to the town, which I should find tiring.'

Edward acquiesced in her plan as he often did when he saw that it meant much to her, though he could never refrain from registering the pain it caused him when they differed. Rhoda felt a certain uneasiness that was not occasioned by his pain so much as a troubling awareness that she had been less than straightforward, not only with her husband, but with herself.

After he had ridden away, she announced her intention of walking to the school. Her cousin, Eleanor, aware that Edward had entrusted Rhoda to her care on the assumption that she would take the trap, protested, ''Tis much too far.'

'It is only a matter of seven miles in all,' Rhoda replied. 'You would think nothing of a walk twice as long.'

'I am sure that had we told him, Mr Jory would have been pleased . . . '

'I do not wish to put Mr Jory to trouble on my account. I simply wish to see the school,' Rhoda answered haughtily.

Later, making preparations in her room, she remembered the bedroom in which she and her sisters had slept as children, how cramped it had been, and guessed that Harold and Eleanor had moved into that room in order to accommodate herself and Edward in greater comfort. She felt shamed by the generosity of their hospitality.

She went down to the kitchen, where Eleanor was issuing instructions, looking as flustered as if she were to be absent for a week instead of a matter of hours.

'Might I have a word with you, cousin.' Rhoda was all meekness now.

Eleanor followed her into the hall, worried by the possibility of further demands.

'My dear Eleanor, I am so sorry. In my eagerness I have been very selfish. It is asking altogether too much to expect you to accompany me. I shall be happy to go on my own. Indeed, I am not very good company of late and shall probably do much better on my own.'

But too much had now been set in motion for Eleanor to call a halt; it was quite beyond her to think of what must be undone were she to change her plans.

So it was they set out.

'The way across the moor is the most direct,' Eleanor said. 'If we follow the path by the river it will be easier but it will take twice as long.'

'I should much prefer the moorland walk.'

They took a stony path that climbed between banks of velvet brown bracken. A kestrel wheeled overhead and a few long-horned sheep cropped the turf around a twisted, wind-torn tree. Above, the sky was grey-washed, with the faintest pink in the underbelly of cloud. Rhoda breathed deeply, the isolation coming to her as a benison. After the fever of the night, this uncluttered expanse cleared her mind and refreshed her spirit; just as she had told Edward it would, she thought, essaying a little self-justification.

Gradually, as they climbed, the land to the east began to flatten out into a great stretch of tussock grass with here and there water gleaming in peaty hollows. On the other side, there was a steep fall to a narrow valley, a sullen, brooding place.

Eleanor remained quiet, not wishing to intrude on her cousin's thoughts. Rhoda seemed to her to be 'very deep', a description she bestowed on any person who dipped into the mind before speaking and was sparing in what was brought forth. Eventually, it was Rhoda who spoke, pointing to a few cottages that hung high above the valley.

'Why would people live in this lonely place? One shepherd's cottage, I could understand, but there must be three, if not four, dwellings there.'

Eleanor stopped in her tracks like a horse confronted by danger. 'Oh, my dear soul! I should 'a thought.'

Rhoda, imagining some household task not covered by instructions, clenched her hands and resigned herself to disappointment. 'Would you like us to go back?'

Eleanor was looking at the cottages, the roofs of which

were not far below where they stood. ''Tis little use now, since we've come upon it.'

Rhoda, coming to stand beside her, saw far below slate-grey water and a huddle of men around a tower-like structure with a tall chimney to one side.

'The mine!' she exclaimed. 'But Edward told me that man probably lied to claim the reward.'

'They'll not give him the money till they find the body. He'd know that – he's fly, Jem Harker.' They stood for a few moments watching the activity beneath them. Eleanor said, 'I reckon that if he says he saw Jarvis up here that night, that's the truth of it.'

'What was he doing himself?'

'Bit o' poaching, that'll be why he didn't come forward till they offered a reward.'

'But what are they doing now?'

'Didn't Edward tell you? The mine's been closed for some years; there's a lot of water down there. They've sent for a diver from way over t'other side o' the county.' She began to cry. 'Oh, 'tis a judgement on me.'

'Eleanor, how can you possibly say that?'

But the more Rhoda tried to console her, the more wild Eleanor's protestations became. Rhoda, at a loss to know how to handle the situation in which she now found herself, was relieved to see a man and a woman standing outside one of the cottages.

'Come,' she said. 'I am sure these good people will let you rest for a few minutes in their home.'

The cottagers were startled by the sudden descent of the two ladies and only with some reluctance led them into the sitting room. Although the cottage itself was not mean in comparison with agricultural dwellings, it had lapsed into a state of decay. It distressed Rhoda to see the squalor to which these people had been condemned. From the little that the man said in answer to her enquiries she gathered that when the mine closed the area had been abandoned by the mining company, but this couple, who had run out of energy or hope, had stayed on. They had come from Wales and said there was nothing for them back there. He picked up whatever work he could and mumbled something about 'over to the blacksmith'. The woman spoke little and cast constant glances out of the window. They both seemed fearful, not knowing what this sudden activity might mean for them, as though by their very existence here they had been discovered in wrongdoing.

When they heard the sound of voices coming nearer, the rattle of falling stones as men came up the steep slope, Rhoda herself suffered acutely the feeling of wrongdoing. This was a terrible moment, something on which she should never have intruded, making herself an embarrassment to all. The expression on the face of the constable who came into the cottage expressed that embarrassment only too clearly. He stopped, his head thrust forward as he bent to cross the threshold, staring at the two ladies; water dripped on to his boots from a bundle he carried in his arms, a bundle clumsily tied up in tarpaulin.

Eleanor was sick, and only years of schooling her body for Edward's sake enabled Rhoda to fight back the bile that rose in her throat. Beyond the door she heard Jory's voice, 'What is it, man?' The constable moved forward with his burden and the moment that Rhoda would have given almost anything to be spared was upon her. She had no idea which of the many emotions struggling within her – horror, contempt at her own weakness, a plea for forgiveness – registered in her eyes. In Jory's eyes she saw the shock of recognition, as though the whole complex of her emotions had been revealed to him. She felt herself known as never before.

The constable had recovered himself. 'I need a cupboard, or a room with a good strong lock. This'll have to wait here until we fetch the magistrate and Doctor Burton. And no one bain't to go near it.' He followed the miner into the back of the cottage, where his voice could be heard giving further instructions.

Rhoda said to Jory, 'We were out for a walk . . . we had no idea until we saw the mine below us.'

The words were of no significance; she was beyond the orderliness of words. If Jory replied she was not aware of it; her mind seemed incapable of interpreting the signals her body was receiving. There were other men in the room now, including the diver, who was ill as much from the fumes in the mine as from his discovery. The miner's wife was attempting to minister to him and to Eleanor. The matter of brewing tea seemed suddenly to assume an importance out of all proportion to other events, and Jory moved to the kettle on the hob while Rhoda went into the scullery in search of crockery.

'This is a terrible thing for you to venture upon,' Jory said when he joined her. His face was a muddy colour, the nearest it would come to pallor; there was purple beneath his eyes and blue around his chin.

'You are sure . . . ?'

'Yes. We opened the sack.'

She gave a little gasp and he turned to her. A pulse beat in her throat, like something trapped beneath the skin. He remembered the sensation he had had as a child, holding a trapped bird in his hands, the tenderness it had aroused in him. He put out a hand and touched her shoulder and the bird fluttered within his own body.

She said, her voice shaking, 'I shouldn't have come here, it was wrong of me . . .'

The miner's wife came in, supporting Eleanor, who wanted to wash her face and hands.

The tea was strong with a brackish taste. Rhoda could drink only a little, but Eleanor appeared somewhat revived by it, although still tearful. It was obviously advisable to get her away and Jory said he would walk back to the farm with them.

'We shall do perfectly well now,' Rhoda assured him. 'And you are needed here.'

'There is nothing for any of us to do here until the doctor and the magistrate come, and I shall be back by then.' As he saw that she regarded this as an imposition on him, he added, 'And to be truthful, a good walk and fresh air will not come amiss.'

The awkwardness between them made conversation difficult, but they were relieved of the necessity to make an effort by Eleanor, who engaged the parson's attention, still wretched with guilt. 'I was angry with him because he owed Mrs Tibbs money for the child's keep.'

'That's natural enough, it was a great burden on Mrs Tibbs, having Jarvis and the child lodging there.'

'But no matter that she grumbled mightily she could never speak really sharp to him, and I don't suffer that way.'

'Jarvis needs someone to speak sharply to him, it is the only way to get anything into his head.'

'Not that I care about him; they can string 'm up the moment they lay hands on 'm, for all I care. But I can't bear to think o' that little one. I can see her now, so proud in her little pinafore that Mrs Tibbs made for 'er.' She began to cry vigorously. 'No one had ever been kind to that little mite afore.'

Jory said, 'Hers was certainly a harsh life.' There was a reserve in his manner and Rhoda thought he was not naturally sympathetic to weakness in women. She said to Eleanor:

'When we get back and you have had time to recover yourself, we will visit Mrs Tibbs. She will need all your kindness at this time.'

Jory looked past the two women, out to the moor, and Rhoda saw sadness of a different order in his face and realised it was this extra dimension of sorrow rather than lack of sympathy that separated him from Eleanor. His eyes seemed to seek for some distinguishing feature out there on the featureless moor, and she thought that he was not only sad, but baffled.

Eleanor, calmed by Rhoda's suggestion of a visit to Mrs Tibbs, now walked with the brisk determination of one who has a duty to perform.

'The pace is not too much for you?' Jory asked Rhoda after a while.

'I like nothing better.'

'Nevertheless, I think we should stop for a moment – it

is the one place on this path where you can glimpse the Highstone.'

It took more than a moment before she could see the stone like a thumb print on the sky. There must have been many better viewing points, but the pause was welcome although she would not have admitted it, and she listened gratefully to his discourse on the probable significance of these ancient monuments. Edward would have insisted on underlining her weakness, yet Jory, so forceful and passionate in comparison, affected not to notice it while creating this opportunity for rest. She had heard that his wife had died in childbirth and that the child had not survived. How sad it was that a man who could exhibit such surprising consideration should find himself alone; the more tender instincts, in a man as strong as Jory, could so easily be blunted for want of use.

'And now you know all about menhirs.' He was aware of her inattention and was looking at her in amusement. This gentle teasing gave her a thrill of excitement, not only for its intimacy, but because his risking it seemed to suggest that he perceived hers to be a more robust nature than most people imagined.

But the moment of lightness passed as they neared the farm and, each in their own way, thought of what awaited Jory on his return to the miner's cottage.

'Their lives must have been very different from ours, their circumstances so unbelievably harsh,' Rhoda said, as she and Eleanor crossed the farmyard. She was thinking of the people who had raised the menhir. 'But then, their problems were not so particular. Or is it that we simplify the feelings of people of other ages than our own?'

In her dream, Clarice seemed to be surrounded by fiery heat and she knew it was that very hot summer in the early 1960s. 'I must breathe deeply,' she told herself. Gradually, the deep breathing produced an almost hypnotic effect. Summer eased into autumn and the heat seemed to relax its grip.

It was a calm, early autumn day. Occasionally brown leaves fluttered past the window, but the great beech tree still shone golden in that same sunlight that slanted on the wall opposite Clarice's desk. The desk, of modest proportions, was not in the centre of the room but occupied one corner; Clarice did not like to be dominated by paperwork. The room was high-ceilinged and spacious; its dignity and the pleasant autumnal scene beyond the window gave a feeling of harmony and acceptance. Clarice, who did not consider herself yet to be in the autumn of her life, even if high summer had passed, thought that she might come to be settled in this post. Sometimes, when she was particularly alive to the impossibility of awakening the vacuously pretty faces that turned to her at school assembly like so many cosseted pussycats, she was aware of compromising herself, of a failure in communication, a sense of a gift withheld. But the awareness lessened as the years passed. Perhaps her restless nature was changing and the time had come to put her ambitions as a painter to one side. She might even grow into one of the great headmistresses. At least, if she couldn't do that, she would become patient with her lot, willing to cultivate her garden; she would put on weight, move, ponderous with wisdom, become wrinkled and benign.

The reverie was broken by a tap on the door. Her secretary, Miss Heffernan, announced that an old girl had called. She gave the name, but Clarice at that time was not listening attentively. She was preparing to ease herself into her new role, be gracious, strike just the right note with a young woman who was no longer a pupil. The girl would go away and tell friends, 'Out of school she's so warm, so approachable, one could simply relax and enjoy . . .'

She did not remember the young woman who came in. Twenty-three perhaps, she thought – before my time. She had a general impression of cinnamon. Brown hair, fawn skin speckled with freckles, pouched lids above eyes you had to look at twice to decide the colour – hazel, probably grape-green in some lights. A hard face, not brash, more a matter of lack of softness. A face that made calculations as of necessity. She looked round the room much as the fire officer might, assuring himself that there was more than one exit. She wore a tobacco-coloured suit and a cream blouse, and looked well turned out but not as if it gave her any pleasure.

'I'm Gillian Davies.'

'Of course, we have your sister.' Why 'of course'? Anyone less like Teresa one could hardly imagine. The telephone rang. It was the secretary asking if tea would be in order.

Clarice said, 'Certainly.' She put the receiver down. 'Will you excuse me a moment – something has just

115

cropped up that I need to attend to. You will take tea, won't you?'

To her secretary, she said, 'Gillian Davies. Is there anything I should know about her? She doesn't look as if she's come to make a courtesy call.' Usually, it did not worry her to be caught unawares; she quite enjoyed the challenge.

Miss Heffernan, who, Clarice sometimes thought, knew everything that had happened since Abraham led his family out of Ur of the Chaldees, said, 'Second of four girls. Eldest is a nun now. Gillian left before taking her A levels; she's a personnel manager at one of the big London stores, I forget which.' Clarice thought she hadn't forgotten, she simply didn't think it important.

'The third child is Coralie, am I right? A family of clever girls who tend to disappoint academically, although we have hopes of Teresa. Anything else I should know?'

'If there is, I expect she's going to tell you,' Miss Heffernan said reasonably.

Gillian Davies was sitting staring out of the window at the beech tree which Clarice thought one of the glories of her view. It did not appear to give the young woman much satisfaction. She waited until Miss Heffernan had put down the tea tray and departed before she turned her head.

'You know my parents?' She spoke with the inappropriate brusqueness of the emotionally ill-adjusted.

'Yes, indeed.'

Dr Davies was a much respected, if not entirely loved, local doctor – too clever to be loved. Clarice had no difficulty in bringing him to mind. He was a man who established an immediate and somewhat uncomfortable *rapport* with his companions. In a dark, merry face, the eyes seemed to see through the disguises of the flesh. Clarice felt all her organs on display under his scrutiny. But there was a certain air of hilarity about him that robbed his appraisal of severity, even of seriousness; it was as though he were saying, 'Life and death are one tremendous joke, possibly in bad taste, but this is the best life we have on offer, so make the most of it.' His wife, not sharing his humour, had settled for invalidism, to which she was wholly dedicated.

Gillian Davies said, 'Coralie's going to Canada at the end of the year. When she goes, he'll start on Teresa.'

Clarice poured tea and handed cup and saucer to Gillian. She also gave her a plate and put another plate, with biscuits, on the table near to her. While she did these things, they could hear the sounds of girls' voices on the playing field, the sharp blast of a whistle, sounds that punctuated Clarice's days here and gave to them a reassuring sense of the continuity of all schooldays. When she had settled herself, Clarice said, 'What is it you're telling me?'

'I can't put it plainer than that.'

'I think you will have to.' She was aware of the coldness of her voice. How sick was this young woman? And if sick, then why?

'The priest knows. He'll tell you if you ask him. He won't be betraying a confession. We've both talked to him about it, Coralie and I.'

'This is a very serious accusation.'

Gillian Davies looked at Clarice; it was a look that

combined destitution and indifference and there was no debating with it. Even so, Clarice was surprised that she should so readily accept that Dr Davies's dark humour might embrace evil. She said, 'How long has this been going on?'

'You'd have to ask Felicity that. Sister Benedicta. She's in France and she won't talk, anyway.'

'Why have you come to see me now?'

'I said: Coralie will be going away at the end of the year. He's never touched Teresa. She seems to have got on better than the rest of us.'

Only a few minutes ago, Clarice had said to Miss Heffernan, 'We have hopes of Teresa,' as though it was a matter of no great moment. Now, hearing again the voices on the playing field, it seemed that Teresa, so light of heart, so gifted, epitomised all the hope that older generations invest in the young. She said, 'Does Teresa know what you are telling me?'

Gillian Davies thought about this, lowering her eyes. She had sandy eyelashes. The eyebrows were scarcely visible. Perhaps it was this absence of lines of demarcation that made the face seem so lacking in animation. As Clarice recalled, the mother was somewhat similar. They seemed both to have been subjected to that technique used in fantasy films when a ghost or an illusion is introduced to create an impression of the unreal, something not flesh and blood. Clarice disliked her and wanted to disbelieve her.

'We're not very close as sisters. There are big age gaps between us, four or five years. I have a theory we represent the times when our mother allowed access. But I think

Teresa knows things go on that she doesn't understand – or want to understand. And he makes it easy for her. She's his favourite, very like him in many ways. He doesn't want to spoil her. They're friends. I can remember when he was a friend to me. He's good at it.' She sounded quite dispassionate, no hint of nostalgia there.

'Why have you come to me?'

'Where else could I go? Our mother? She's been no more a mother to us than a wife to him. She's not really ill, you know, it's a convenience; something that gives her dispensation from the necessity of becoming an adult. She spends a lot of time at the convent and when she's not there she recites the rosary. My father is quite brilliant; he could have gone a long way in his profession. But he had to be mother and father to us when we were young.'

From what Clarice remembered of Mrs Davies on her rare appearances at the school, this portrait, though unpleasant, could well be true to the subject.

'Your priest?' she asked. 'What about him?'

'It would split the parish and the bishop wouldn't like it. He might help if someone else did something, got things going – otherwise he won't.'

'What do you mean by "got things going", Gillian?'

'She could be sent to a boarding school, couldn't she? I know a girl who was sent to boarding school the first time her father laid a finger on her. But her aunt was a JP and very tough. Coralie thinks you're tough, too.'

'Why didn't she come with you?'

'She won't talk about it.'

'She talked to the priest.'

'That's different. She knew he wouldn't talk.'

'Gillian, you're saying that neither of your sisters will talk about this, that your mother . . . I'm not sure what it is you're saying about your mother, but I don't get the impression she would admit anything. Have you any idea of what you would have to face if you pursued this allegation, of the pressures on you from which neither I nor anyone else could protect you?' Or, she thought, looking at the face with its sick distaste of life, the impression you would give under cross-examination. Whatever she might have suffered, this young woman was unlikely to arouse sympathy, did not, in fact, appear to want it.

Gillian said, 'I don't mind much what happens to me.' Again that indifferent tone. 'There's not much anyone could do that would be worse than what's already happened.' Clarice could see her at the stake, saying, 'Light your bonfire, I can hardly wait,' and not touching any hearts.

'Then what do you want?'

'I want to save Teresa, of course. It's just that I don't know how to set about it.' She looked surprised that it should be necessary to say this, and for a moment there was something in her face that suggested that if a course of action were to be mapped out for her she would be prepared to go through the fire.

And can I do less? Clarice asked herself. It sounded extravagant, but when one reflected on it, faced with such a story and believing it, could one do less? Well, of course, one could be sensible. One could consider the reputation of Dr Davies and make comparisons that could only be unfavourable to this unappealing young woman. But

Clarice had had an upbringing that had not laid much emphasis on being sensible. Her father had had common sense, but where his political sympathies were concerned he rather regretted the passing of the days of the Tolpuddle Martyrs. Her own headmistress, Miss Wilcox, had had little political zeal, but Clarice had no doubt how she would have responded to this situation and it was with a flood of gratitude, a sense of awakening, that she said, 'I'm no more sure than you how to set about this, but I promise you I will do something.'

The next day she made a few tentative enquiries.

She tried Miss Heffernan first. Miss Heffernan said, 'Things can't be good in that house. You have only to look at that woman.' The members of the staff to whom she spoke reacted in much the same way. If anything was wrong in that house the culprit was Mrs Davies. Clarice allowed herself to go as far as floating a suggestion. 'She may well be the root cause, but surely Dr Davies . . .' They took her to be referring to a mistress. Dr Davies would have too much to lose by any impropriety, they asserted, and anyway he was not that kind of man. A number of the staff were elderly women who had devoted their lives to teaching — not much scorched flesh there, Clarice thought, or understanding of it. They really believed a man did not endanger his career simply for sexual gratification. Clarice wondered how they managed with history lessons and English literature. But then Antony was a licentious Roman and Parnell was an Irishman, whereas Dr Davies was a respected local doctor known to them all. And why should she sneer at them? She had never suspected anything herself. Probably the most successful secret society in the world is the close-knit middle-class family.

Only one teacher, the music mistress, seemed to hold her eye a little longer than was necessary before she said, 'No, I don't know of anything that might be troubling Teresa.'

'You have no reason to wonder?'

'No.' Again, thoughtful.

'If anything should give you concern, even something quite small, would you let me know?'

'Yes, of course.' She seemed relieved, whether because the matter had been put to one side, or because she had been offered an opportunity to re-open the subject, Clarice could not tell. This was a rather touchy woman and she thought more might be gained by leaving it at that for the time being. But as she turned away, the woman said, 'She isn't singing so well – doesn't seem able to loft her voice so effortlessly.'

'Have you talked to her about it?'

The woman looked away. 'I think perhaps she may feel she'll miss Coralie.' Whatever else she knew, she would not say.

Clarice turned to the only person to whom she felt she could speak frankly.

The moment she began to relate details of her talk with Gillian Davies to Robert Havelock she knew she had made a mistake. Disquiet made her tense. She had wanted to talk quietly, reflecting on the situation as she laid it before him. Instead, she was aware that her manner was unsympathetic, her voice brusque. She watched the contours of the familiar face she so loved change as mystification gave way to astonishment, not so much at the tale Gillian had told, but at her acceptance of it. The geniality was stripped away like topsoil, revealing a much harder substratum. The furrows in the cheeks deepened and the strong lines set around the mouth; the eyes that had so often laughed into hers filmed over. She was reminded that the Border Country had formed him. His mother had been an Armstrong and it amused him to say that he came of a reiver family. 'You would never have been so ruthless,' she had told him and he had said, 'Make no mistake, had I lived then I'd have been a rider.' The eyes that looked at her now might well have witnessed those turbulent times.

He said, 'I trust you haven't told anyone else?'

'No, that's why I've come to you. I need help in handling this.'

'Handling it?' He raised his eyebrows and she saw that he was furiously angry. 'In what way do you have to "handle" this?'

'I have to do something,' she said on a rising note.

His voice was icy. 'You do realise that by doing something with this calumny you may destroy that family? Certainly, you will destroy the very innocence you seek to preserve.' He spoke incisively and she could sense that he was distancing himself from her, standing back to get a clearer view. It was as if, in this one brief conversation, their love was being replaced by dislike and she was watching it happen. He had enjoyed their differences; his was a strong personality and he had no need to fear dissension. Her quirkiness he could accept; her unease in the job had made her vulnerable, and that he had liked, too; even her comments on her colleagues he could respond to, he relished saltiness in a woman. But a certain steely quality of mind he had never found attractive. He had tolerated it in her because he was seldom a target and we all overlook the blemishes in the beloved. Now he saw her stripped of all the pleasurable trappings and imagined himself confronted with the truth of her. He was repelled.

But she loved him every bit as much for being himself at this moment. She was desperate to keep him.

'I know you're right,' she said. 'The danger is of causing more harm than has already been done. That's why I've told you and no one else. I badly need your advice.'

'You've had my advice.'

'Robert, I know that Malcolm Davies is a great friend. But Teresa is my pupil. You know her as well as I do. She's young and eager and full of promise, one of the most lively, unusual children in the school . . . '

'And if she weren't full of promise, a pudding of a child, what then?'

'And if the wife were sympathetic and engaging, what then? Let's say I am as attached to Teresa as you are to her father.' She pulled herself up. 'Let's not say anything of the kind. Whatever the circumstances and however much we would prefer not to know of this, once known, something has to be done. It is inconceivable that this lovely child should be spoilt.'

'What is inconceivable is that you are ready to believe there is any question of her being spoilt. The wife is an hysteric and Gillian, too, no doubt – she was always singularly unappealing. For some reason she wishes to hurt her father. And for a story like this to get around would be sufficient. A doctor is very vulnerable. Have you any experience of how people's lives can be ruined by vicious gossip?'

'No, I haven't, have you?' The words flashed out before she could control her tongue.

'Quite some experience, in fact. Don't forget I grew up in a small Scottish village. The Free Church minister, whose wife was a harridan, enjoyed the company of one of his congregation. It was totally, pathetically innocent, amounting to no more than his escorting her home from evening service, never even setting foot inside the garden gate, let alone the house. But bitter spinsters who had never even enjoyed that much pleasure in their lives got to work. For those few brief moments of happiness he was hounded out of his living.'

He himself had done far more to deserve con-demnation, but Clarice, who felt the less guilty, was not sensitive to this and came in too impatiently.

'This is different, Robert. It's his daughter who makes the accusation, and the eldest daughter became a nun.'

'I appreciate that you're a Quaker, but let me assure you that not all convents are full of abused women.'

'And Gillian says the priest knows.'

'He would never betray the secrets of the confessional.'

'I don't think there's any question of that. She says she and Coralie have spoken to him. Father Damien is your priest. I hoped you might feel you could have a word with him.'

'If you think I will be party to this kind of witch hunt, you are much mistaken.'

'It doesn't have to be a witch hunt. Teresa could be sent to boarding school.'

'And you're prepared to meddle in other people's lives as the result of an unsubstantiated allegation?'

'Made by his own daughter. She's telling the truth, Robert. If she wanted to cause trouble for her father there would be better ways of going about it than telling her priest and coming to me.'

He was not listening and she realised it was the allegation itself that affronted him. He saw quite clearly the devastating effect it would have on his friend and his instinct was to defend him. The question of the truth of it was not something he was prepared even to consider.

He said, 'I'm indebted to Malcolm Davies. He's been a good friend to me – to us, as it happens.'

'You mean, he knows about us?' The unholy glee she sometimes glimpsed in the eyes in that dark face assumed new meaning.

'Don't worry. He would never betray a confidence.'

'No, he enjoys them too much.' It was on the tip of her tongue to say she would rather he had confided in anyone but Malcolm Davies, then she recalled that she had discussed their affair with a woman whom Robert disliked. She felt herself becoming entangled in a mesh of conflicting emotions and loyalties which blurred the issue so that the clarity of the main outline was lost. The centuries had bequeathed to the man she loved complex ideas of honour and betrayal, justice and indebtedness. He was someone of whom it could be said: a good man to have at your shoulder in troubled times. She was confused and rather frightened.

'Can we put this behind us for a time? I can see I may have rushed at it. In three weeks I have to take a party of girls to France, Teresa among them. It will afford a breathing space, a time to reflect.'

A time to heal the breach, she hoped. But when she left him she carried heavy in her stomach a pain for which she knew there would be no healing. She sat in her office after she returned to the school, hearing the voices of the girls as they came back from the playing field, cheerful as they anticipated weekend pleasures. Then cars started up as, one by one, the staff took their leave. Miss Heffernan had left early to take her mother to the doctor. Soon the cleaners moved in, their raucous voices echoing in the empty building. Clarice wished she had planned a weekend away. But where would she have gone? Her parents were dead, her affair with Robert had left her with little time for women companions, most of whom had drifted out of her life. She was suddenly aware of how lonely she was, how unfriended. 'Once known, something has to be done.' Brave words when spoken as a rallying cry to all good men and true. But alone? She was not at all sure she was strong enough for what lay ahead of her.

She went to the window and pulling up the sash leant out. It was cold and already the fallen leaves were curled, dusted with silver. The sky was streaked with tufts of pink and saffron that, as she watched, spread and darkened into a deep crimson glow. The air was acrid with frost and woodsmoke.

Fourteen

CLARICE SAID to the woman with the lamp who sat by her bed, 'I'm sorry. I'm very sorry . . .' What she was sorry about was not clear to her, but she seemed to have been saying it all night.

The farmer's wife said, 'I've brought your breakfast. I thought you'd prefer to have it in bed. We've had a Dutch party staying the night. It's a bit noisy in the dining room, everyone talking about farming methods.'

'I'm so sorry.' There she went again. She watched the farmer's wife clear a space on the little table by the bed, then fetch the tray she had put on the chest of drawers. She could have sworn there had been a woman with a lamp there a moment ago. But now that the curtains were drawn back and sunlight swathed the end of the bed in a warm haze she realised she must accept the loss of a companion who, she sensed, understood better than she herself what was happening. It must be late, after nine o'clock, with the sun riding high, well established up there.

'What happened?' she asked dully, not really wanting to know. 'I'm sorry to have given you this trouble.'

This time the farmer's wife heard her. All those other sorrys must have been directed to someone else. Heaven alone knew there was enough to be sorry about.

'You fainted last night at dinner. Don't you remember? You kept saying you were very hot, but you didn't seem to have a fever.'

Clarice elbowed herself up in the bed. Her head was heavy and she felt unsure of her body, as though something had broken down somewhere along the assembly line.

'I'm so sorry,' she said. 'Was I a nuisance?' Being a nuisance was the eighth deadly sin.

'No, of course not. You gave us a bit of a fright, though. Dr Hillman came over; he reckoned you'd be all right after a good night's sleep. You don't remember?'

'I'm afraid not.' Other things had occupied her wandering mind and whatever had passed between her and the doctor had been lost.

'I have a bit of trouble with my heart,' she said, hoping this explanation might serve as cover for any misdemeanours she feared yet to come. 'Nothing much, of course. We've all got something at my age, haven't we? Bits and pieces that wear out.'

The farmer's wife acknowledged high blood pressure. 'Nothing much, though.' They looked at each other in complicity, both women who would never admit to anything more serious than 'nothing much'.

'Dr Hillman said he'd come again this morning. They're not expecting you at the theatre. I had a bit of trouble explaining to your director. Is he deaf?'

'To everything but *Pericles* at the moment.'

'I'll send Carrie up in a little while to see if there's anything else you need.' As she went out of the door, she said, 'As long as I've got my senses, that's all I ask.'

129

But I haven't got mine, Clarice thought. Not any more.

She ate as much of the breakfast as she could manage and made her usual apologies to Carrie, who went away giggling. Outside, the children were playing the murderous games children so enjoy. How distant their world seemed, much, much further away than that of the woman with the lamp, who had looked as if she cared more than anyone had cared since Clarice's mother died. 'I'm sick and I want my mother,' she told herself. 'I conjured her up.'

At eleven o'clock the doctor called. A brisk man, but thorough in his examination. He told her she should rest today. 'Nature's warning,' he said as he left. 'Nature's warning, Miss Mitchell.' Clarice believed him; her path lately seemed strewn with warnings.

After lunch, Alan came. 'They're all very worried about you,' he assured her.

'Not half as worried as I am.' She didn't want to talk about the company, she had other company on her mind. 'I dreamt again last night. Have you got a few minutes?'

He said 'yes' cautiously. He wasn't happy in the world of dreams, feeling he had enough problems without interference from his subconscious.

'I want to tell you about it because you'll understand,' Clarice informed him firmly. 'It wasn't a dream. When you do a performance, it's not like a television repeat, is it? Each performance, it happens again – Hamlet sees the ghost, kills Polonius, remembers poor Yorick . . . '

'What did you dream?' Alan asked. Hamlet had associations for him on which he preferred not to dwell.

'Gillian Davies came to tell me about her father. It wasn't memory or a reminder: it happened. Another performance, you might say.'

'Was anything different?'

'How would I know? I wasn't observing, I was there, in the action. But yes, I suppose there was one difference. In life, mercifully, we are usually allowed to take our trials bit by bit, in stages; we don't have to absorb the whole shock at any one moment. It's a cumulative effect. You're given time to grow into your particular harrowing. But in my dream, my body felt the whole of it, the full impact – not my mind, my body.'

'You probably aren't doing your body any good by dwelling on this,' Alan said.

'It's not my body I'm worried about, it's my mind.'

Clarice felt she was achieving something in the recounting of the dream experience, but she was not sure what. It was like one of those maddening episodes in detective stories where the character senses that a conversation contains a vital clue but can't bring it to the forefront of the mind. The solution was usually to let it lie awhile and then it would pop to the surface. She was content to rest on her achievement even if she didn't know what it was.

'I'm sorry.' Yet again! 'Do you ever think you're going mad?' she asked Alan, in a hurry to bring her mind to order. 'You must have done, I suppose, when the police came and dug up your garden.'

Now, there was something to be sorry about. Poor Alan, why was it his problems were never treated seriously? Perhaps it was that in spite of his undoubted ability to portray tragic characters on stage, in real life he seemed destined to play a melancholy clown.

'It was so unreasonable,' he said. 'I told them that I buried all our dogs and if Mrs Percival had only cared to ask me, instead of phoning the Chief Constable, I should have been perfectly willing to show her Marcus's corpse.' The mild resentment sounded fresh, as if it had been stored up waiting for someone to release it. Clarice recalled that at the time the director's one concern was the staging of *Hamlet*. She remembered his trying to ascertain, not very capably, whether Alan's 'trouble' was likely to prevent his appearance. Neither he nor Alan had wished to use the word arrest and the conversation had ended with Alan saying he hoped to be available.

'When I told the police I didn't know where Muriel had gone, they behaved as if there was something unusual about it, whereas in my experience it's quite common in these circumstances not to leave a forwarding address. I'm quite an expert on the subject, after all. Muriel took off on a number of occasions and she never told me where she went.'

'Didn't you ask?'

'What good would that have done? It wouldn't have altered anything if she'd said she'd gone to Torquay. But that wasn't the worst of it. "Would you say, sir, that your marriage was a happy one?" And then they expressed a sort of pained surprise because I didn't seem to know, as if the idea of a marriage that was less than happy was something quite new to the police. One might have thought this was Puritan England of centuries ago.'

'Was that when they dug up the garden?'

'Soon afterwards.'

Why hadn't they talked like this before, she wondered. 'Alan, it must have been dreadful for you.'

'They didn't even offer to pay for the returfing.'

She hadn't known him well then, had only worked with him on a couple of productions. When they came together, they were too bruised by their experiences to want to rehearse them to each other. At least, she had imagined him to be bruised. 'Were you afraid they would arrest you?'

He looked away into a corner of the room as if his mind needed a dark place at this moment. 'Do you know what I was really afraid of? That they would find her; that perhaps I had killed her and somehow overlooked it. It's surprising how much guilt we seem to have stored up in us, isn't it, waiting a chance to get out? I can remember standing at the window watching them, dreading what they might turn up.'

'Did you hate her?'

He considered this, as he might have done a weather front that had failed to live up to his forecast. 'I don't think so. She was very tiring to be with all the time. One of those people who must have a reason for everything they do. When we went for a walk she always wanted to know where we were "heading for", while I didn't want to head anywhere in particular. She must always have an object in view, while I'm a fairly objectless man. But I don't think I hated her, not really . . . ' He looked at his watch.

Clarice said quickly, 'I killed someone.'

'No, Clarice, no, it wasn't your fault.'

'I brought about a death. It's the same thing.'

He looked at his watch again.

'Never mind about rehearsal.'

'But we're doing a run-through and they can't start without Gower, he's the prologue.'

'Damn the prologue, we're long past that. We're well into Act V and we need to talk.'

'Clarice, you should rest. The doctor said so.' He kissed her gently and she let him go. When he had gone out of the room, she said:

'I killed a man.'

This brooding was hardly what the doctor had intended when he advised her to rest. She looked around for something to occupy her mind. The prompt copy of *Pericles* lay on the table beside her and she decided to read it straight through, thinking about the play instead of the actors' lines. The producer had said the play was about loss and reconciliation, a theme which spoke to her condition. When she came to the scene in which Pericles discovers the long-lost Marina she began to cry, gently at first. Then as she read,

> 'Give me a gash, put me to present pain;
> Lest this great sea of joys rushing upon me
> O'erbear the shores of my mortality,
> And drown me with their sweetness'

she was torn by rending sobs until it seemed her ribs must crack, her body fall apart. By the time she got to Thaisa's appearance she was in calmer waters and fell asleep, the book open on her chest.

It was dark when she woke. She felt better than might

have been expected and decided to go down to dinner. The nooks and crannies and alcoves that comprised the dining room were filled by the Dutch party, two of whom sat at her table. They exchanged pleasantries. Clarice asked what farming methods could possibly be common to Holland and this untamed area, and they told her that they were doing a tour of the West Country on their way to the Isles of Scilly. The farmer's wife, who was serving, said that next week a party of Frenchmen were coming. 'With them, we have more in common.'

As Clarice was drinking coffee, Alan called to say that there was to be a technical rehearsal the next day so they wouldn't be needed until the dress rehearsal in the evening.

'I thought you might like to go for a walk and stop for a pub lunch.' A pub lunch was not something he favoured on walks, so this was an acknowledgement of her weakness.

'Unless there's anything else you'd rather do? A trip to the coast?' He looked absently into the middle distance while she digested this offer, prepared to sacrifice himself, though hoping it might not be required of him.

'I'd like the pub lunch.'

They started off before nine in the morning. As they walked across the farmyard they could hear sounds of hysteria from the nearest barn; the *Crucible* company had started rehearsing early and was about the business of witch-hunting. Backstage staff were assembling near one of the other barns, looking long-suffering as only backstage staff can.

'It's like having a day off from school when everyone else is working,' Alan said.

They walked for two hours across moorland and then came down into a valley where a clapper bridge forded a river. It was too early for lunch, so they sat watching the water frothing and frisking about the great gritstone slabs and the sloping stone piers. The river was swollen and no free space showed beneath the arches.

'I'm sorry I had to go to rehearsal yesterday.'

Alan spoke diffidently, as he did when he was not happy with the lines a playwright had given him. Any minute Clarice expected him to complain, 'I'm not sure how I should be playing this scene.' Surprisingly, he decided on resolution. 'You've never talked much about what happened to Teresa, and afterwards. We've always agreed that going over it wouldn't mend anything. So I only know the bare facts. Yesterday, I felt you wanted to talk and I should have stayed with you.'

She sat in silence for some minutes and he didn't prompt her, perhaps giving her time to sort out her thoughts – or hoping she would decide that she no longer wanted to talk. Torn branches of trees lifted above the water like the arms of skeleton swimmers, and looking at them Clarice realised she had reached a stage where her personal inclinations no longer counted; if she didn't talk, her subconscious would break through and plague her with dreams of the drowned Marina. So she said, addressing the gritstone slabs which looked strong enough to endure all things:

'I took a group to France during half-term. Not a strictly educational visit. In fact, I wanted to give them something of what I had in my schooldays, an escape from the straitjacket of orthodox learning. So we went to the

Lot, eight of us in two cars; six girls, all French students, and two members of staff. We meant to walk, explore the villages, perhaps see the cave paintings. But outings were optional. Just being in another country, and one as different as France, would do them more good than any culture trip. One or two of the girls wanted to sketch and paint. Others walked. I went with the walkers, of whom Teresa was one. I knew she had been to France several times with her family, but she was vague about where they had stayed – Vienne mostly, was all she contributed. Her lack of contribution generally disturbed me. Usually, she could be relied on to lift any group she was in and was an ideal person to have on this sort of holiday.'

She paused, looking at the bridge and thinking how strange it was that many people would have lived a lifetime unable to reach the other side of the valley save by this bridge, icy in winter, flooded in spring. Some would have crossed it in fear, others bowed with toil, but a few would have danced across.

'It wasn't just that she was highly intelligent; there was something else that distinguished her from the others. There are some people who seem to be motivated by the sheer will to enjoy life – or something other than will, which suggests an effort, more a natural orientation to joy. Do you know what I mean?'

Alan scratched the side of his nose. 'Not really.'

She thought about this, looking at the shadows of trees moving on the nearer stepping stones. 'It's a gift, one can't emulate it. I think it was there in her father. That may seem a strange thing to say of someone who did such terrible things; but he had a brilliant mind and, I suspect, more than his share of sexual energy. Who knows what may happen when the driving forces in a person are dammed? If things had turned out badly for Teresa, I think she, too, might have been corrupted, her natural gaiety channelled into mischief. She wasn't a plodder on the road to virtue; nor, I think, did she have the moral fortitude to survive the quenching of the light that sparked her spirit. I believe she sensed some danger in herself – not to herself, but from herself.

'She wasn't helpful on the journey out, nor was she considerate to the girl who was car-sick. Usually, she responded spontaneously to other people's needs; now she seemed unaware of them and behaved as though she were the only person in the car. This self-imposed isolation, I felt, surprised her as much as the rest of us. After we arrived at the *pension* where we were staying I had a few minutes alone with her as we were unloading the car. I said something fairly trivial, like, "You don't seem yourself, Teresa."

'I can see her now, nodding as at a point reasonably made. She said, "I'm afraid there's nothing I can do about it." It was a flat statement, neither defiant nor apologetic, an acknowledgement that she had no means available to her of tempering her behaviour. One of the other girls came out to help and I decided to wait until I had more time alone with her.

'On the fourth day we stayed in one of those French villages that spill down a hill, a clutter of oblong buildings like so many dominoes. Scrubby hills around, mountains on the skyline. We went for a long walk and as we came home towards evening the clouds were gathering and to the west the sky was a deep lavender. Did you notice what I said? "We came home." I said it quite naturally just as the thought came to me then, that feeling I get in those old French villages of a homecoming. It isn't nostalgia but the essence of all homecomings.

'The sun shafted across the village, caramelising all those higgledy-piggledy buildings; something touched my cheek, soft as a bird's feather. I thought it was for me, that moment; I didn't realise until afterwards it only brushed me in passing.

'That evening at supper she came to life again. She was never someone who had to hold attention by mono-polising conversation, but she could convey an intense interest in her companions that heightened an occasion. On this evening that is what she did, as though she had something precious to share with us.'

She bent forward for a moment, rubbing her fingers through her tangled hair as she gathered herself for something she was now almost too drained to tell. When she spoke it was as if she was relating something to herself, bringing it into being.

'It was a warm night for October, but I don't think that explains why I went out into the little yard at the back of the house in the early hours of the morning. She was there, in a stone archway leading on to the side street; only a shadow in the moonlight, but I knew it was her.

'I said, "Teresa, come back." ' No authority, just a plea.

'She said, "Give me a few hours, Miss Mitchell, please."

'I stood there in the yard and watched her go. I heard her footsteps in the street. Then the cloud covered the moon and it was pitch dark and I thought this is madness.

I felt my way towards the arch and out into the narrow street. I could neither see nor hear. I went back. The member of staff I shared the room with was still asleep and I didn't wake her.'

She clasped her hands around her knees and bowed her head. Alan knew how to hold a pause and he held this one a long time before he asked:

'How old was Teresa then?'

She straightened. 'You may well ask. She was thirteen. I let a thirteen-year-old girl walk out into a pitch black night in a French village a long way from any town and I didn't report her missing until the next morning.'

Alan was silent, considering this. Eventually he said, 'I think that was rather a brave thing to do.'

'It was wildly irresponsible. I've never been able to work out since whether it was one of those things that's meant to happen and I was merely the instrument, or whether it happened as a result of a flaw in my character. At the time, I had to assume it was a flaw in my character and I resigned. In that I'm sure I was right – as well as prudent, since I would have had to go anyway; it was obvious to myself and everyone else that I was not fitted to be in charge of young people.'

'But did they know you saw her go?'

'It was a question they never asked. I often wonder when I read the reports of enquiries how much goes undetected because the right question is never put. Robert, of course, guessed. But he wouldn't betray me – after all, he was indebted to me.'

'And the governors?'

'They wanted someone to blame and said that the

arrangements for supervision hadn't been adequate. I sympathised with that.'

'Did her family have any idea of where she might have gone?'

'Who can tell? They certainly weren't going to. The mother became, if anything, more dissociated. And, as you know, her father committed suicide. Gillian went to see him; what she may have said, or threatened, I can only surmise, but it was shortly after that visit he hanged himself. He was a doctor, he must have known gentler ways, but he hanged himself.'

'And nothing has been heard of her since?'

'Nothing.' She got up abruptly, flexing stiffened muscles. 'I don't want to examine how I feel about that.'

He stood beside her and put an arm round her shoulders. 'You did your best, Clarice.'

'God help anyone when I do my worst.'

'At the time, though . . . '

'Oh, at the time, I knew. In that moment when we looked at each other, she was already a dark form, her substance lost to me. Had we talked all night, it would still have come down to that plea, "Give me a few hours, Miss Mitchell, please." I knew I had to let her go. But there are consequences. I've lived with the consequences ever since, Alan, and I can no longer be sure it was something other than an act of madness on my part. In my darkest moments I can even persuade myself that she wanted me to stop her.'

'Have you ever been back? I know you've been to France – we went together once. Did we go to that village?'

'We passed through it.'

'There was one time . . . '

'I don't want to say any more; there are some things I can't talk about.'

He could accept this easily enough, as he accepted most things. He wasn't really curious, just showing willingness to provide what comfort lay within his power, confident she would not ask for anything beyond his capacity for giving. But he loved her in so far as he was able and felt some lingering uneasiness.

'Is there something you're afraid of?'

'I've said I can't talk about it.'

He saw that if he pushed any further there would be unpleasantness of one kind or another.

'Pub lunch.' He pointed to where, across the bridge, people were making their way to a small hotel on the hillside.

'Where did they all spring from?' Clarice asked.

'They've come from the fair, I expect.'

'I don't know that I want to get caught up with fairground people,' she said, uncharacteristically apprehensive.

'There aren't that many of them. We shall find a table on our own. And it's not swings and roundabouts, more of a craft fair. I thought we might have a look on our way back.'

After lunch, they went to the fair, which was on the heath, and Clarice bought scarves for Christmas presents. Alan bought her a sweater that she had admired. At one booth people were having their faces painted, not only children; Clarice watched, aware once more of a certain uneasiness. She remembered going to a fair in France and the fear that suddenly one of the bizarre figures would swing round on her and it would be Teresa. Then the figure would dance away and she would never know whether the girl was simply playing a part in the carnival, or whether she had changed dreadfully.

On the way out, a figure did swing suddenly into her path. A bright, sun-warmed face smiled not so much at her as through her. Alan caught her arm as she stumbled. 'What is it?'

'A woman. I keep seeing her. She's getting older.'

'Aren't we all?' he said absently.

Visibility was poor on the moor. Green turf threaded its way between clumps of heather down tracks that dissolved in murky haze. A shining grey car parked on the turf looked spectral, as if it had landed from another planet. Clarice, following a little behind Alan, said, 'She still doesn't see me.'

Fifteen

JOAN HAD been to the fair. She sat in the yard, taking off her boots to relieve her swollen feet. The wind parted her hair at the nape of her neck and blew chaff in her face. It was autumn and the wind already had winter's breath on it; Joan's face glowed where it had caught her cheekbones. The old servant watched her from the kitchen door.

'We were afeared something had happened to 'ee.' She had not really been frightened, it was her way of rebuking Joan for taking a long time. 'Mistress warned 'ee to leave early. Always robbers about when people are returning from the fair.'

'I haven't been to a fair for years,' Joan said, bringing her purchases into the kitchen. 'There was so much to see.'

The old woman began to check the articles before putting them away in the cupboard that she guarded closely.

'There was a man with a performing bear, Martha. The bear mauled him.' It had brought the performance to an abrupt end, otherwise she would have been back even later. 'There was a madwoman came to the fair when I was a child. She used to dance through the village street.'

The old woman said, 'You've forgotten the ginger.'

'There wasn't any.'

'You're a liar.' She went into her store cupboard and brooded over the omission of the ginger. 'I don't know why she took you in.'

'We are related,' Joan said indifferently.

'Related! I've served her for thirty years. I was with her afore she ever went to be with the Duchess. And I never heard any mention of 'ee.'

'My mother was a Twynyho. Ankarette used to visit us years ago. Plump and rosy, she was, and she wore a yellow kirtle. I can see that kirtle now . . .'

'Oh, you can see anything you set your mind to, and she'd believe anything, she's so good-natured. It was the priest got her to take you in, telling her some story that moved her kind heart.'

'All this fuss about ginger.'

'She does so love a touch o' ginger,' the old woman adopted a crooning voice, as though talking to a child. 'Apple tart wi' ginger I was going to make for her, because she's been so sad since the Duchess died and she came back here.'

The wind sent dust and bits of straw eddying into the kitchen. 'There was a juggler, too,' Joan said. 'He was so funny, I laughed until I ached.' She pressed a hand to her breast as if the laughter and the ache were still there. 'Oh, Martha, doesn't it stir you, an evening like this! All sparkling, and the wind . . .'

'I don't have no time, me dear. And, anyway, I'm too old. Little bit o' peace is what I want, not stirring up.' She looked at the other woman, her wrinkled face neither friendly nor particularly hostile. Never going to be young again, she thought, but comely enough, even in her

145

thirties. Something wrong there, though. Never settle will this one; she'll be moaning and crying out at every turn of the wind, no good to herself or any man. And she'll know no more about life the day she dies than the day she was born.

Joan said, 'He was a lovely man, the juggler . . . '

'They're bad folk, those wandering people. Bad folk, all o' them.' She went past Joan into the yard and hauled herself up the steps to the loft that was above the kitchen. Joan could hear the timbers creak.

Martha called out, 'Will 'ee get that washing in afore dark?'

Joan loitered in the yard, throwing up pegs and trying to catch them as the juggler had done. While she was doing this a noise of which she had been half aware became more definite. 'Horses!' she called out. 'Just fancy, Martha, more than one horseman riding this way.' She listened as the distant thrumming became distinct and metallic. 'A fair and several horsemen riding by! And all in the one day. Can't ever have been so much happen here afore.'

But they weren't riding by. Suddenly, they were in the yard, five men splendidly mounted.

'Is it the bear?' Joan cried out to one of them, who seemed too fine to be concerned with a runaway bear. She was holding the sheet in front of her, stretched out, half-folded. Perhaps in the dusk he did not see her. He swung down from his horse and went towards the kitchen, where Martha was now standing, clasping a basket full of apples.

'Where's your mistress?'

'What do 'ee want with 'er?' Martha's voice quavered.

The other men crowded after the first man, pushing the old woman into the kitchen. Joan dropped her arms and the wind folded the sheet gently around her limbs. She heard the sound of heavy boots on stone, overturned furniture, Martha's voice, further away, not like she had ever heard it before. 'I tried to stop 'um, Mistress, I tried . . .'

None of the other servants came running out to see what was happening. Memory triggered fear. Joan freed herself from the sheet and ran into the kitchen, through the narrow archway into the hall. Men were coming down the stairs, one of them had Ankarette slung over his shoulder, she was clutching at the stair rail and screaming, her mouth a gaping hole in her face. Martha was lying at the top of the stairs, her head was tilted back sharply over the top step and her mouth was open in a bloody grimace. Joan knew that she was dead.

'What's this? One here we missed.'

A man had turned back. He was standing with a foot on the bottom step, looking up at her. Behind him, someone called out and he half-turned; in that moment when he was off-balance Joan rushed past him into the kitchen. He recovered soon enough and came after her, but she had managed to grab a warming pan from the hearth and as he lunged towards her she swung with all her might, hitting him between the eyes. She was a strong woman. He lay still where he had fallen, but to make sure, she hit him several times.

The table had been overturned and the apples from Martha's basket rolled about under her feet. She picked one up and ate it while she put on her boots. Then she sat, hunched forward, shivering as if she had the ague. After a time she was conscious of movement out in the yard. She picked up the warming pan and turned towards the door. There was a man standing there; she could see a horse behind him laden with baggage. His face in the light of the lamp that he carried was white as flour. He whispered hoarsely, 'I heard terrible screaming when I was some distance away.'

'They took my mistress,' Joan said.

He nodded, apparently needing no convincing. 'They were in the town,' he said, 'asking for someone. The Duke of Clarence's men. 'Tis said she poisoned the Duchess of Clarence.'

'She was good and kind to me.'

He came towards her and she moved back to let him into the kitchen. It was the juggler from the fair, a small, wiry man with bandy legs and arms as long as a monkey's, not very lovely at close quarters, but with some gentleness about his puckered face. He looked around the kitchen and then walked towards the hall; as he passed the upturned table he saw the man lying there. Joan, who was feeling faint now, took another apple and stood by the open kitchen door, looking out into the darkness, glad of the cool of evening.

'Did you do that?' His face was more green than white now.

'They took my mistress away and they killed old Martha.'

There was blood on her hands, she noticed for the first time; it was all over the front of her gown, too.

'You must be very strong.' He looked at her respectfully.

Then, becoming businesslike: 'You'd best get him out of the way. It won't help your mistress if they find him here.'

Joan said, 'Where can I take him?'

'There's a river yonder, across the field.'

The juggler found rope in the loft and tied the dead man's hands and feet together to make it easier to carry him; then they humped him out into the yard. 'I'd put him on my horse,' the juggler said, 'if it wasn't for the blood getting over everything.'

So they carried the man down to the river which was full and rushing crisply over the boulders. When they had pushed the body into the water, they washed their hands and Joan rubbed down her gown. ''Tis hardly dried, so maybe it won't stain,' she said. The water was very cold; some of the coldness was inside her now and she was shaking more violently.

'There'll be his horse,' the juggler said. 'I reckon we could sell his horse and no questions asked; a horse isn't like a dead man.'

It took them some time to catch the horse which had strayed; as they crossed the field, cajoling softly, Joan thought, 'I can't go back, so I suppose I'd better go with him, since that's what he seems to have in mind.'

'I killed a man, Lady.'

'Do you think she really killed a man?' Dame Priscilla asked.

'That's a matter for the priest,' Dame Ursula said wearily. 'He seems to think she's harmless.'

'Don't turn from me, Lady. They took my children away and I didn't know what I did after that.'

Sixteen

As she drew up outside the church, Clarice thought, I seem to be in and out of lives other than my own. There is something I am being told that I don't want to accept, it waits for me, like a patient presence.

The church was in the village of West Bentham, which had not appeared to be signposted. Perhaps if she had come another way it might have merited a mention, but she doubted it. In this area, she had discovered, signposts tended to deal with places at some distance, such as the town of Mellor; the near-at-hand they disdained. Local people, when available, seemed uninterested in place names. She supposed that at one time villagers must have remained in their tiny communities with little knowledge of the outside world, even of what lay on the other side of the hill. Or did the fact that the area was sparsely populated mean that in the distant past people had moved from place to place, not settled, led a wandering life? These were not idle speculations. It was as though she were tracing her ancestry, or that of an acquaintance – two acquaintances, in fact, one deeply rooted, the other, Clarice guessed, rootless.

She looked at the noticeboard beside which she had parked her car. St John the Evangelist: Vicar, Rev. John Moxey. The church itself was partly hidden by a short avenue of trees; to its right was the vicarage and to the left, the village school. As far as she could see, this was the extent of West Bentham. But here, as elsewhere, appearances were deceptive, because soon parishioners began to arrive, some by car, but a number on foot, springing, it seemed to her, out of the very hedges.

As the bell began to summon the faithful, Clarice experienced a reluctance to join them that had nothing to do with religious scruples. She enjoyed the Anglican services she attended from time to time, only wishing that if they felt it necessary to sing they would do it as wholeheartedly as the Methodists. No, this reluctance was more the wish to prolong the state of uncertainty which had so plagued her of late and which now seemed unaccountably to have become wholly desirable. Already she was beginning to regret the impulse that had led her to make an appointment with the vicar.

The bell had stopped. She got out of the car, impelled by the strongly held conviction that it is bad manners to be late for any meeting and particularly one of a religious nature.

The graveyard was a tangle of grass and wild flowers dotted with seedling hollies, but the graves were well maintained. She had a brief glimpse of the church as she approached the porch, a sixteenth-century building much subject to Victorian improvement. Inside it was rather dark, the plaster having been stripped from the walls by the restorers. The windows were plain glass but the surrounding trees, even at this time of year, blocked the light. She sat in the side aisle. To her left was a board in the shape of a scroll naming past incumbents as far back as

1589. She noted that the present vicar had been here since 1965 and that his predecessor had ministered from 1934 until 1965. Prior to that, priests had come and gone rather frequently until a Thomas Jory, who held the record, being minister from 1842 until 1890. It was the man before him who would be most likely to have known Mrs Tresham, née Carey, who was born in one of the farmhouses in his parish. She read the name: Samuel Naylor. It meant nothing to her. And the church itself, pleasant and well cared for, reasonably well attended and boasting a small choir, gave the impression of being cheerfully unconcerned about the past. The language was modern, pedestrian but inoffensive; small children scampered up and down the aisle, watched with mild disapproval by a black retriever accompanying his blind master. It was probable that Miss Wilcox had attended a service here and that her grandmother had been christened here, but if their spirits still lingered, they certainly weren't making any contact today.

Clarice recalled how people would say of a place, 'The very stones cry out,' to which she invariably replied: 'Not to me, they don't.' Today was no different. Whatever it was she shared with the nineteenth-century Mrs Tresham, it had nothing to do with susceptibility to psychic phenomena or the awareness of the language of stones. And why, she wondered as the congregation settled for the sermon with the sound of falling foliage after a departing wind, should she expect to gain any particular impression from sitting in the same building that had once been visited by the Careys and their descendants? Had not Mrs Tresham written in her diary that she, Clarice, was a ghost? This might suggest that it was in the future rather than the past that they encountered each other. Some little annexe of the future reserved . . . for whom?

She forced herself to attend, but sermons seldom engaged her mind, probably because of her preference for her own opinions to those of others, and she soon found herself studying the man rather than his words.

The vicar was in his fifties, she judged, and had that wry air of failure which she found endearing in clergymen – to her Puritan spirit a successful clergyman was an abomination. When he smiled, a not quite quenched naivety lit up his face; a man who could not cure himself of the error of expecting rather more than God was pleased to give him? She thought, made sombre by a little sermon of her own, that perhaps there were gifts that God had wanted to give us had we not been quite so concerned with our misconceptions of what was good for us. Suitably chastened, she rose to add her croak to the singing of 'Be Thou my vision, O Lord of my heart'.

When the service ended and people began to move towards the porch, she walked round the church, looking at the memorial tablets, none of which enshrined members of the Carey family. The pulpit was interesting, with a Jack o' the Green among the carvings, leaves and acorns surrounding the face of Silenus.

'Unusual, surely, as late as this?' she said to the vicar when eventually he joined her.

'Yes, it is. We're rather fond of him, though some visitors raise eyebrows. They don't mind him peering through foliage somewhere up aloft, but they don't like him looking out at them from the pulpit.' They walked out into the churchyard. 'I seem to remember that he figures in one of your paintings.'

Clarice was charmed, and wishing to repay him with some little compliment of her own, she said, 'I see you've managed to retain your village school. That's a real achievement.'

'And, I may tell you, we had to fight for it.' She had sparked his pride. 'Came very near to fisticuffs once or twice.' He paused, looking fondly at the building. 'We've added a bit to it, of course, but it's still the monument to one remarkable man.'

This, it transpired, was the long-serving Thomas Jory, who was obviously something of a hero to the vicar. Clarice, respecting enthusiasm in others, realised she must listen patiently while he recounted the history of the man who had pioneered education in the area.

'He was a prodigious walker, too,' the vicar said when he had almost run out of attributes. 'He thought nothing of covering thirty miles in a day.'

'So I would be wrong in thinking that people scarcely moved out of their villages?'

'Certainly. They would all have walked long distances, the men particularly. Though I expect you're right in thinking they would have known little about the people in neighbouring villages. On the other hand, bad news seems to have travelled fast enough.'

He went on to tell her of the murder of little Ellie Jarvis. 'That soon seems to have spread around the moor. Thomas Jory had a lot to do with the apprehension of the man, Will Jarvis. A terrible tale. The child was done away with for the sake of the two shillings and six pence a week it was costing the father to keep her.'

'Where did they find the body?'

'You aren't familiar with the story?'

Clarice wasn't, but she had an idea that she knew the answer to her question. The vicar said, 'There's an old mine shaft up on the moor, not so very far from here.'

The grim little story had stemmed the flow of his enthusiastic account of the life of Thomas Jory and he turned reluctantly from contemplation of the school to lead her into the vicarage.

'They have some little ceremony for the children at the Sunday School, so I'm afraid my wife can't join us.'

Clarice murmured politely. He opened the door to the sitting room, a big, forbidding room that seemed too lofty to reward any attempt to make it look homely, although efforts had been made with flowers and crookedly hung pictures, mostly too small to give colour to the walls.

'Very difficult to heat,' he said. 'One can hardly bear to think of Jory alone in this barn of a place all those years.'

Clarice, who did not want to waste any more time on Parson Jory, said, 'It's very kind of you to see me, and on a Sunday of all days. But as I explained, we have so many rehearsals . . .'

'Ah, yes. Now, you must tell me what I can do for you.' He went to a small cabinet. 'You will take sherry?' he asked hopefully, and Clarice, suspecting this was an indulgence he seldom permitted himself, said that she would.

Once seated in a lumpy armchair she found that the urgency that had driven her here had lost its sharp edge and the fear which had accompanied it was dulled. But the vicar was smiling at her expectantly and as he had given up his time to see her, she must do her best to cobble up a reasonable explanation of her intrusion.

'As I told you over the phone, I'm staying at the Carpenters' farm. It so happens that the grandmother of the headmistress of my school was born there and my headmistress – Miss Wilcox – used to stay at the farm, in the twenties and early thirties.' He was looking uncertain, as well he might, unsure of the drift of her mind. She decided to dispense with story telling.

'Roberta Wilcox had a great influence on me.'

He warmed to her immediately; if she wasn't careful they would find themselves discussing Jory again. But she did him an injustice; it was she he was concerned with now and he said gently, 'A journey of discovery, perhaps?'

He sees an elderly woman evaluating her life, seeking answers in nostalgia, she thought: well, let it be.

'Or perhaps there's something more?' He was more perceptive than she had given him credit for and sensed that his first conjecture had been wide of the mark. Clarice, too, found herself better focused.

'Mrs Carpenter showed me old Mr Carpenter's diaries. We looked through them together and found several references to Miss Wilcox's visits. It seemed she was interested in finding out more about the Carey family, but they weren't able to help her. One of the entries referred to a visit to the parson, who it was felt might have more information. I wondered if you might have any records?'

'You could certainly look at the parish records, but I don't imagine that's what you have in mind, since it's Miss Wilcox in whom you're interested. I'm afraid St John's hasn't produced a Kilvert or a Parson Woodforde. In fact, my immediate predecessor was a man who seemed to suffer from a great disinclination to set pen to paper.'

So that was that – or was it? He was turning the stem of the glass on the table beside him, concerned with some evaluation of his own. When he looked up, he said, 'Your headmistress's mother would have been Mrs Veronica Wilcox, am I right?'

Clarice found her throat dry and her voice was husky when she replied, 'You're better informed than I. I simply know that her mother came here sometimes, but I had no idea of her Christian name.'

He said, looking down into the glass, 'She used to visit old Jory right up to the time he died and she brought her children to see him, though your Miss Wilcox may not have been born until after his death. I know this because I came across letters she wrote to him, very affectionate letters, telling him all about her school and the subjects she was studying. Later, she wrote about her family. Jory's wife died in childbirth and he never married again. I imagine this correspondence must have been a great comfort to him, and it seems, from what she said, that he was the best kind of confidant, able to share both her excitement as learning widened her horizons and the joys of her parenthood.'

There was silence in the room. Clarice pressed her fingers against trembling lips.

'Yes,' he said. 'I found it very moving myself.'

It was some moments before she could trust herself to speak and he waited, perhaps a little perplexed by the extent of her distress.

'The letters?' she said eventually.

'They were in an old trunk in the attic; it looked as if someone had emptied out a desk and stuffed the contents into it, perhaps intending to go through the papers sometime later and then forgetting. I burnt them. They were not what you might call confidential, but they were the private letters of private people and no concern of anyone else. Perhaps you disapprove?'

Clarice shook her head. 'No, I hope I would have done the same.' The room no longer seemed large, was, in fact, getting far too small each second and her unruly heart was crying out for more space and fresh air. She got up and the room contracted further. 'You have been very helpful and I mustn't keep you any longer.'

He accompanied her to the door and then, as she made to go down the path, he said, 'You might be interested to see Mrs Tresham's grave.'

'Mrs Tresham?'

'The grandmother you mentioned. One of the sad things that came out in the letters Veronica wrote when she was still a young girl was that her father was so deeply grieved he was unable to talk to his daughter about her mother. Jory, it seemed, was the only outlet for her feelings of love and loss.'

'And Mrs Tresham is buried here?'

'Come, I'll show you.'

He led her through the long grass to a row of gravestones near the churchyard wall. Clarice knelt down and, fending off the branches of a holly, she read:

SACRED

TO THE MEMORY OF

RHODA

BELOVED WIFE OF EDWARD TRESHAM

DIED 29TH SEPTEMBER, 1857

She remained unmoving, staring at the headstone. The vicar looked at her speculatively; graves can have a strange effect on people, but her comment when it came can hardly have been what he expected.

'But that is this Thursday.'

Seventeen

G OWER, THE story-teller, was bringing the play to an end:

> 'In Antiochus and his daughter you have heard
> Of monstrous lust the due and just reward:
> In Pericles, his queen and daughter seen,
> Although assail'd with fortune fierce and keen,
> Virtue preserved from fell destruction's blast,
> Led on by Heaven, and crowned with joy at last.'

In the gap between her cubbyhole and the tabs, Clarice could see the faces of the children in the front row, eyes round as marbles. They had looked like that when the play began and enchantment had held them throughout. The rest of the audience seemed to have shared something of their wonder, for they reacted with more than polite enthusiasm when the players took their bow.

The side door was open and she could see the director standing out in the yard, as redundant as Prospero after he renounced his power.

'A real success, I think, don't you?' she said, joining him.

They could still hear the applause. The cast would be taking their third curtain call by now and, however great the encouragement, would not take another, milking the audience being regarded as a mortal sin by most Theatre Guild companies, second only to the appearance on stage of the director.

'You've lost them now, haven't you?' Clarice said, hearing the cast making their way to the dressing rooms, laughing and embracing stage-management staff as they went, shouting thanks to the wardrobe mistress and her assistants.

'When I went into the dressing room before we went up half of them looked at me as if they couldn't remember who I was; the others pretended to be delighted to see me. I can never decide which is worse.'

'It's a bit like that with a painting,' Clarice said. 'When there's nothing more you can do, it breaks away from you, stands on its own.'

The audience was coming out in twos and threes, briefly outlined in the doorway of the lighted theatre before disappearing among the shadows of the yard. In the dimly lit auditorium someone was going round with a dustpan and brush, collecting discarded sweet wrappings and tickets, making ready for the next performance. On the set the assistant stage manager was sweeping the floor.

'Gower, Pericles, Marina . . . theirs is the only reality,' the director said sombrely.

Clarice protested, 'Oh, come!' without conviction. As they turned towards the backstage entrance, she said, 'Four more performances. Do you ever find yourself being afraid that one day something quite unforeseen may occur?'

'In my experience,' the director said grimly, 'it nearly always does.'

Eighteen

I

AT THE crossing of tracks, in a place where the wind pressed cold against the cheek and stung the eyes, and surged on thrusting through invisible barriers with a noise like tearing silk, an old man, grey-bearded, walked with firm, measured tread, staff in hand, watched impassively by horned sheep. Above, the sky was herring-ribbed with cloud beneath which darker smudges moved fast. In spite of so much motion, there was an underlying stillness that was not disturbed by intrusive wind and racing cloud.

The old man stopped at the crossing of tracks and considered. In front of him ground fell away rapidly to where, between a line of mop-headed trees, there was a glimpse of squares of green, tidily hedged, surrounding the small town of Mellor. Sunlight flickered pale and ghost-like on its stone buildings as if strained through gauze. Behind him, and on either side, the moorland gazed contemptuously down on this tranquil scene.

Cattle, large, black and ponderous, occupied the downward path, in no mind to hurry. At the side of the track sheep drank from a pot-hole. The old man strode forward, using his staff briskly to make a way between the cattle. The wind surged on, leaving the stillness untouched.

II

Joan and the juggler were travelling to Mellor. She was lighting a fire and he had led the horse down to a stream when a party riding close by stopped to watch. A pompous red-faced little man who bobbed about on his horse like a cork on a rough sea began to describe her activities. 'And now you will notice, she will lay that stone so, leaving a well in the centre . . . ' Joan followed his prompting and succeeded in getting a good fire going. She hoped he might stay to cook the fish for her, but by this time his companions were eager to be on their way. There was a youth among them and he threw a coin to her.

'He was very handsome,' she told the juggler when he returned.

'It was his clothing and his mount you thought so handsome. Were I dressed as he is able to dress you would think me very handsome, too.' And he began to show her how splendid he would be, his hands moving surely over flowing robes, showing the fullness of wide hanging sleeves, making her feel the softness of a fur border; drawing attention to the contrast between the rich, heavy cloth of gold of the gown and the soft satin sheen of its lining. As he moved, splendid raiment swayed about his thin, bony body.

Joan clapped her hands and cried, 'And the jewels! Show me the jewels!' There were rings on his fingers, a brooch at his throat and another on the cap he wore on his head. 'Oh, you are indeed handsome!' she said. In her

163

heart, she thought, ah, could we but live like this all the time. He seemed composed only of joy and laughter when he acted, and yet when the performance ended care seeped into every line of his wrinkled face. He was like Martin, more gentle and undemanding, but worried, worried all the time about where they would sleep and how they would get food.

'We could take a chicken,' she pointed out.

'That is stealing.' He would rather starve than steal. 'If I am caught stealing they will cut off my hands. What would I do without my hands?' It was his constant nightmare that he would have his hands cut off. Sometimes she stole without telling him. After all, if she didn't have hands no one could expect her to wash clothes, kindle fires, and cook.

She was disappointed to find that even on the road care kept her company. She and the juggler had been together for many years now and her face had been roughened by sun and wind, the dry flesh scored by fine lines. She had lost that heedless delight which had so tormented Martin, but the grey eyes were still wide with the candid surprise of one who is slow to learn life's lessons and the parted lips found a smile less effort than composure. But her mood could darken, and now, as she watched the juggler ravenously eating the fish, she said:

'He was but a boy.'

The juggler looked at her and looked away again. He knew by the drawing together of the features that the mood was on her.

'He was like my son, very beautiful. In fact, I think he was my son; he recognised me and that was why he made me a gift. He is very rich and he owns land that stretches in all directions.'

She sat hunched, holding her arms tight around her stomach, bowed as if in pain. It was like being with child again, the thing struggled so within her. But this creature found no natural way out; year in, year out, she must carry it, tearing and rending. Sometimes its labour ceased and it seemed to withdraw to a secret place where she could not reach it, but it was always there.

'I hope they are kind to my boy,' she shouted. 'Else I'll have them whipped.'

'Now that is beautiful stitching,' Dame Priscilla said. 'Aren't you pleased at how beautiful it is?' She knew that pleasure in one's achievements was very wrong, but there was no one but Joan to hear her say it, since Dame Ursula had succumbed to the sickness.

III

Edward Tresham had taken Rhoda and Veronica into Mellor, where they had stayed for two days. This was an expedition he had set his heart on. It was inconceivable that in the course of his enforced stay with Rhoda's relatives he should not spend some time in the one town which was of any interest to him − the seat of a noble family whose castle, he had ascertained, might by arrangement be open to those wishing to view the portrait gallery and the armoury. In order to realise his ambition he was prepared to subject himself and his family to rigours he would not have permitted in any other circumstance. He was aware that Harold had been doubtful of his ability to handle the wagon and was pleased, not to say relieved, at the way he had acquitted himself. On a journey of some three hours they had encountered little traffic; the hazards lay in the waywardness of the tracks they must follow. But the sedate old horse had lived a lifetime on the moor and was well versed in meeting its challenges and, provided he could go at his own pace, could be relied on for safe transport. Edward, more sensitive to the whims of animals than those of his fellow humans, allowed him his vagaries, patiently enduring stops while he drank from peaty hollows or inspected, and was inspected by, his moorland cousins.

On their return journey, they stopped at a field gate to eat the food the innkeeper had provided for them. Here the horse found succulent nourishment in what appeared to be a rather thorny hedge, and Edward the opportunity for discourse. Above them lay the moor and beneath was spread out a great tapestry of green and brown and blue, field, river, hamlet and distant town. Sitting with his back to the moor, Edward looked down into that ordered landscape and said, 'This is what God created out of chaos.'

He talked of purpose and pattern, of the harvest of the centuries which incorporated change and development, new agricultural methods and improved forms of transport, the canal system and the wonders that would come with the construction of railways. 'We are remaking Eden,' he affirmed in a rare moment when feeling and intellect were at one.

Rhoda, listening to him, thought, 'And the people who

have lived here, what of them? They, too, must be part of this pattern, a stitch in the tapestry, myself included.' Together with the awareness of pattern in the land, of how it gathered together all of history, there emerged the concept of a person who was, child and woman, Rhoda Tresham, with a life that was not a disconnected series of episodes but one in which the sadnesses and failures, the disappointments and longings, the contradictions and seemingly unrelated impulses were all of a piece, leaving nothing to be discarded. Could it be that the way back to Eden required the wanderer to come bearing the fruit and scars of experience? If this was so for her, then the same must be true for the two women who kept her company and whose scars seemed sometimes to itch beneath her own skin.

'Roberta!' their daughter exclaimed in triumph.

'What are you talking about?' Edward asked, startled.

'She's talking about her family,' Rhoda explained gently.

'What family?'

'I'm always telling you, but you're not interested. I'm going to have lots of children, seven at least, but I couldn't think of the name of the youngest and it suddenly came to me. She's Roberta.' She scrambled from the wagon and went to impart this news to the horse, who nuzzled her shoulder.

'The new school will soon put those ideas out of her head.' The day had turned sour for Edward. 'In fact, if what I hear is true, she will probably lose the ability to bear children.'

He was morose on the long ride across the moor, which

looked at its most bleak and forbidding, the sky grey and a mean wind blowing. It was two in the afternoon when they drove through West Bentham.

'That will be Mr Jory's school.' Rhoda pointed to a squat building in a clearing where trees had been cut down recently. Faintly, the sound of children's voices came to them, raised in unmelodious song. Her eyes moved towards the church, wondering whether at this moment he might be there, sitting in a side aisle as she had seen him once before the morning service, his face composed in prayer or meditation. The trees in the graveyard moved in the light wind and suddenly she experienced the warm, healing release of tears; yet it was not she who cried.

'I shall send Roberta to that school,' Veronica announced, and proceeded to chant, 'And Nathaniel and Rudolfo and Hortensia and Gunhilde and Sylvester and Etheldreda and Marmaduke . . . '

'There would seem to be some advantage in being the last,' Edward commented drily.

'And Nathaniel begat . . . '

'What about John or David?'

'That would be very dull, don't you think.'

She went to sleep planning the second generation of her family.

When they arrived at the farm they found Jory had walked over from West Bentham and was talking to Harold and Eleanor. Veronica was very tired after the long journey. 'She'll need her bed, poor lass,' Millie said. She prepared a dish of porridge for the girl, who thought it odd to have porridge at night but ate it without complaint.

When she and Rhoda were in her bedroom, Veronica said, 'Has the parson come about the little girl?'

'What makes you think that?'

'Because then I never see him. You won't let me into the room. And I like to see him. He knows some wonderful names and he doesn't mind hearing about my family.'

'You think about your family now, my darling. By the time you've got to Gunhilde begat . . . you'll be asleep.'

But as she lay in bed and Rhoda adjusted the lamp which must be lit in case the child woke and was frightened, as she so often was, of the dark, Veronica whispered, 'Did he really kill his daughter?'

Rhoda sat on the edge of the bed, smoothing the sheets. 'Do you worry about it? If you do, we must go home. Is that what you would like?'

'It won't make any difference, will it?' Veronica said with that uncomfortable logic of which children can be capable. 'The little girl will still be dead.'

Rhoda, having no answer to this, said, 'I love you, darling. And your father loves you.'

But Veronica had perceived there was badness in her world that a loving mother and father could not put right. She began to recite, 'And Nathaniel begat Justinia and Rudolfo begat . . .' But she was not asleep by the time she got to Roberta and it was an hour before Rhoda went downstairs.

Whatever had been said in the parlour had tired and tried them all. Eleanor was talking about the child. While her voice recounted excitedly incidents of great pathos in the innocent life of Ellie, Edward sat rigid with rage, knuckles gleaming white on knotted fingers. Harold looked uncomfortable in his chair; at the best of times the farmer scarcely knew what to do with his body when indoors and now he looked as if he might break loose and run at any moment. Jory, in contrast, was still and Rhoda was aware of that reserve she had noted before when Eleanor spoke of Ellie's fate.

Edward, greeting his wife, said, 'Apparently, while we were staying in Mellor, they brought Jarvis in. I'm amazed we did not hear of it.'

'They took him at night, quietly,' Jory said. He, too, looked at Rhoda.

'And why did they do that? Why did they protect him?' Eleanor exclaimed. 'They should have dragged him through the streets.'

'He'd not have survived had they done that.' Jory sounded unutterably weary.

'Nor should he! It says in the Bible that anyone who offends one of these little ones should be hanged with a millstone round his neck. Our Saviour didn't say anything about taking them into jail by night and having a trial.'

Harold got up as if his wife's outburst freed him from restraint. He said to Edward, 'Seemingly Millie's gone to sleep out there. While Eleanor sees to tea, I'll see to the horse.'

Edward, who thought he himself had seen to the horse, was only too willing to accept this excuse. 'I'll come with you.'

Eleanor paused on her way out to say to Rhoda, 'When I think o' that sweet little soul struck down in all her innocence, I don't have no charity in me. And I hope that no one's going to suggest I should be the means of persuading his children to visit him. 'Cos I think that would be a wickedness.'

She went into the kitchen, where she set up a great rattle among the pots and pans while berating Millie. Rhoda looked enquiringly at Jory. He passed a hand wearily to and fro across his brow as if trying to restore some inner rhythm to his thoughts. She seated herself opposite to him, waiting. Eventually, he said, 'Jarvis wants to see his children. If it's a means of bringing him to repentance, I think he should.'

'Do you think he does repent?'

'He repents of being caught, that's sure enough.'

He seemed unaware of the pious expressions of outrage and grief that were the normal currency of exchange at such times. What a strange man he was, she thought, and was aware of him looking at her as if wondering how much he could say to her. She trembled inwardly, being unsure of her ability to withstand this test. He was a man capable of deep thought; but whereas Edward's intellectual gifts seemed to drain him of feeling, Jory's presence became ever more powerful as he spoke.

'Jarvis is dissolute, unreliable, dishonest; he is also uneducated, of low intelligence and has no skills. Bringing up a family of four, deserted by the mother, was quite beyond his capability and his pocket. Do you understand what I am saying?'

She shook her head. 'But I can see it is very important to you and that you have thought a great deal about it; whereas my dear cousin Eleanor never thinks at all. She knows instinctively what is due to all occasions, while I, increasingly, know less and less.' But she knew in her bones that she could never accept the killing of this child and her throat constricted with the fear of what might be asked of her.

'I think Jarvis is guilty of a terrible crime and that he should, and must, pay the penalty for it. But his situation was so far from anything I have ever experienced that I find I cannot judge him. Over the last years I have seen terrible destitution, have witnessed people living in such despair with no hope of the improvement of their lot. I have stood by while better men than Jarvis crumbled.'

'I have glimpsed something of this,' she said tentatively, remembering the couple living at the abandoned mine.

'And the child. This is very difficult. Will you listen to what I am trying to say and not translate it into something not meant?'

He looked intently to where she sat, so close to the lamp it was hard to tell whether the glow of light emanated from flesh or flame. Beneath his gaze she felt that more was being asked of her than the words implied and when she nodded her head she felt as impetuous as if she had permitted an impropriety.

'Ellie was not likeable. Far from being innocent, she appeared knowing beyond her years; she lied and constantly provoked trouble and knew how to play on people's bad feelings. Her life was so devoid of good influence one could hardly expect that she would be otherwise. But people who found her unpleasant and did not hesitate to make harsh judgements about her, calling her a "mischievous little baggage", now speak of her as if she were an angel. Mrs Tibbs, far from taking the child to her heart, was constantly complaining to Jarvis about her. It was quite beyond Jarvis to manage her. The pinafore, of which you have heard so much, belonged to one of the Tibbs' children and Ellie stole it. Mrs Tibbs let the child keep it after pleas from your cousin, Eleanor, whose heart is open to the needs of all children, even the unlovable. It is a terrible story which involves us all, because it makes plain to us the extent of rural poverty that is beyond any of us to solve. If we vent all our rage on Jarvis, we have learnt nothing and it will never be solved. And if it isn't, I sometimes fear there will be no hope for any of us.'

This sombre thought was rather beyond Rhoda, whose mind in any case had fixed on something else while he talked. She said in a low voice, 'It makes me realise how little I understand of love; how I confuse it with mere liking.'

He looked at her with an admiration so ardent her hand went to her throat. 'You go to the heart of the matter. Loving Jarvis is not within my compass. But I begin to see this may be a failure in me that I cannot afford.'

Eagerly, he went on to tell her how many times over the last few years he had had to remind himself that the very people whom he scorned were the ones with whom Christ cast his lot. 'We paint sentimental pictures of the poor and rejected in order to make ourselves comfortable with the idea that Our Lord consorted with them, but when we are confronted with the scabrous reality it sickens us. But we must not turn away; for our own sake as much as theirs, we must learn to see Him in these people. If we fail to do that, there is no hope for humanity.'

She listened, astonished that he should share his vision with her, should admit to his own failures and falterings, and she began to envisage dimly what a blessing it would be, what an outpouring of grace, to spend one's life with another with whom one could explore such depths and heights. From this it was but a small step to thinking how she might assist him, support him. His thick hair was already streaked with grey, she noted, and felt its stubbly mat between her fingers as she ministered to him when he was weary. Perhaps she might even give him strength when he was discouraged. And from there the way was open to the forbidden pleasure of how she would best comfort him and he her. She found herself suddenly faint and then he was kneeling beside her.

'I am so sorry, I had no right to talk to you like this, to upset you ...'

'I am all right.' She was unused to the nearness of a man. Edward, for all his love of her, was not passionate or demonstrative. The mixture of masculinity and tenderness in Jory which had already attracted her, now seemed overwhelming.

'No, Mrs Tresham,' he was saying, his eyes warm with concern. 'You are not all right. You have often seemed to me to be deeply unhappy and I have longed to help you and have found it hard to restrain myself from speaking of it.'

'No, no.' She made little gestures of agitation. 'I am a very foolish woman – indeed, you would think me shallow and frivolous were I to tell you ... after the things we have spoken of this afternoon, my troubles ...'

The door swung back and Millie came in with the tea

tray. Fortunately, she had backed through the door and this gave Jory and Rhoda some seconds to compose themselves, she turning her attention to the fire while he cleared papers from the table.

Edward was too angered with Jory to join them for tea and he retired to the bedroom, excusing himself on the grounds that he had correspondence to attend to. Harold was in a hurry to catch the last of the daylight and neither Jory nor Rhoda had an appetite. Eleanor was too upset to take much note of her companions and the meal was soon over.

Rhoda said, 'I will walk some little way with Mr Jory, Eleanor, otherwise I shall suffer from the cramp after so long in the wagon.'

The smell of cooling earth refreshed them after the stale air of the parlour. The dry leaves of the thorn bushes rustled like taffeta. Rhoda was much shaken by her behaviour and would have walked the whole time in silence had it been left to her, but Jory spoke as though there had been no interruption, no interval since the moment when he knelt beside her.

'How can you imagine I would ever see you as shallow and frivolous?' He laid a hand on her shoulder; she trembled but did not draw away from him. Her breathing was fast, a mere snatching for air. On the branch of a tree a blackbird fluted the seconds away, every note pure and unstressed.

'I came to this place because it means so much to me, I thought it was everything, that I could lose myself in the vastness of the moor, that I could breathe again, that I would find freedom.'

He said, 'And then?'

'Then?'

'There's always a then, isn't there? I, too, am much moved by the moor; but I can't live there, I have to go back to my home, ponder upon whatever thoughts came to me as I walked.'

She said sadly, 'I told you I was frivolous.'

'No,' he said urgently. 'It's only that you haven't gone far enough. Can't you see? Moorland is only moorland; it's not a reflection of our need, it's grass and bog, stone and running water. It won't embrace us, provide a refuge — except in death. It would give death all right, if one used it unwisely. The moor is free; yes, I too feel that. But free to be itself, not personal freedom for us. It's all very well for the poets, that sort of thing, but it doesn't solve our problems, help us to live our lives. Whatever Mr Wordsworth may say, one impulse from a vernal wood does not teach us more of moral evil and of good than all the sages can. We can't identify with land, make it an image of ourselves. We are not hewn of this rock.'

The dusk was not dark enough for her at this moment and she averted her face. 'Perhaps it was death of a kind that I wanted.'

'No.' He was vehement in his rejection of this. 'You said freedom, that's the word you used. You have to ask yourself what is this freedom that you need.'

She was silent and after a few moments he said, his voice hoarse as if strained with pain. 'I am sorry. I am the one who is foolish and shallow, suggesting that all problems can be resolved with a little reflection after a long walk. Heaven knows I have walked and walked and found the same problems waiting for me unameliorated on my return home.'

Unequivocally, and with an icy clarity, it came to her: you are the resolution of all my problems. I want the freedom to love you – so perhaps it is not freedom I want, but another kind of bondage. Aloud, she said, 'This is as far as I can go.'

He looked out towards the moor where the last of the light glimmered pewter on the rim of the sky. 'I have been hungry for so long,' he said. 'We must talk again, please.' He turned and took her hands. 'You must see that we can't leave things like this. Will you come to the parsonage soon; whenever you are able to arrange it? I will make it my business to stay there for a day or so. In any case, there is much that I have neglected.' She was looking at him as he spoke, emboldened because it seemed that this might be the last time she would see him, for she certainly could not consent to what he had asked. In the evening light the violet eyes looked huge in the pale face. He touched her cheek with a finger and miraculously, as if he had found a hidden spring, the tears came.

As he took her in his arms she felt something twist and jerk in her stomach. It was as though a stream had been unblocked; it was running through her body when she hurried back to the farm. She pleaded a headache, said she was upset by the day's events and consented to accept the sleeping draught that Eleanor prepared. But during the night the stream was running fast and it seemed it must carry the house away, like the time when the great floods had come with a high tide that had beaten the river back over its banks, flooding whole villages, changing the contours of the land. The water altered the colour of everything; the light, even inside the bedroom, was different, wavering, everything unstable.

IV

The market in Mellor was so full of people it was a wonder any commerce was possible. The traders had set up their stalls in the middle of the cobbled street, leaving scant room for the activities of officialdom. Even so, people gathered to watch as loaves were weighed, eager to see the bakers condemned, shouting abuse irrespective of which way the scales fell. A big, florid-faced man, greatly puffed by his own importance, read out details of prices, weights and measures, standing rather too near the yarn stall for the comfort of the trader.

Chimneys belched brown plumes across the pale face of the sky. Smoke and dung mingled with fresh bread, leather and huddled humanity to make a smell that was as special to market day as the traders' wares. In the narrow alley where Joan had gone in search of food not watched over by a trader, the stench of dunghills was overpowering after the fresh air of the moor. The close, hunched buildings blotted out the sky and for a time she seemed to move in a dark cavern, its sooty walls oozing damp. Then suddenly she came to stables and, beyond, a small courtyard; a door was open and a man was sitting paring vegetables and throwing them into a big pot beside him. He looked as if he might welcome a diversion. Joan told him of her travels and he listened with sympathy. She said

178

that she had lost her husband who had died fighting for King Edward at the battle of St Albans; she had been turned out of her home and left to wander the country. She told the tale tolerably well since some of it was true; she told so many tales she was bound to tell the truth every now and then, even if she did get her battles confused. Over the man's shoulder she could see a long table in the kitchen laid out with newly baked pies and tarts that made her mouth water; above his head there was a ladder leading to a loft.

'Would there be any apples you might spare?' she wondered. 'I do so crave an apple, coming from the country as I do.'

While he went up to the loft, she went into the kitchen and helped herself to as many pies as she could store in the pocket which, in her one gesture towards frugality, she had stitched into her skirt. The servant returned with apples and also gave her half a loaf of bread and a slab of cheese.

She carried her bounty away into the warren of dark streets before he could discover his loss. On the outskirts of town she came to the ruin of a house, a few blackened timbers witness to the fire that had destroyed it. She sat on a low, jagged wall and ate the bread and cheese. The tarts she would leave for the juggler.

Nearby, Clarice ate a bread roll, sitting in the vestibule of a café which was like a dark cavern. The dining area was bright and cheerful, full of pensioners enjoying a day trip. She, however, must sit in purgatorial gloom since she did not want a meal, only coffee and a roll – a compromise of which the establishment appeared to disapprove. She shared a table with a couple similarly ostracised.

Out in the cobbled street people walked aimlessly up and down, peering in souvenir-shop windows or reading menus. There was little else to do since most of the buildings in the street were eating houses of one kind or another. The yarn market, a handsomely restored building, looked too pristine to awaken a sense of a past age, but it provided a welcome shelter from the biting wind and several people were eating packed lunches perched on the low brick wall that would once have enclosed the stalls. The man at her table read from a leaflet for the information of his bored wife, 'Erected at the beginning of the seventeenth century, replacing ramshackle stalls known as The Shambles.' He clicked his teeth at this example of Jacobean discipline prevailing over medieval rough and tumble. Clarice thought The Shambles must have been hell; the humanity here present today was hugger-mugger enough for her.

Yet once, and not so long ago, there was nothing she would have enjoyed more than sitting in a café looking out at an unfamiliar scene. A new town or village, a new street even, triggered her imagination. The place did not need to be beautifully preserved, she did not require it to be free of visitors other than herself; however seemingly mundane, it lay before her, a scene to be savoured. The light will never fall again in quite this way, she would think; the individual composition of this street at this moment will never be repeated. It was the constant awareness of the uniqueness of the fleeting moment, the attempt to touch the quick of life, to capture the changing quality of light, that had fascinated her and was the impulse behind her painting. Now, she had lost the taste for it.

And the theatre, to which she must return for the evening performance, had lost its power to enchant. Last night, their opening night, Alan had said to her, 'I think you'll be glad when this production's over.' In fact, she seemed unable to think of its being over, of packing one's bags and leaving.

'I know we agreed to stay until Monday to see the next production,' he had said, 'but we could go on Sunday morning, if you like. And as for coming down the following weekend to see *The Crucible*, there's no need for us to do that.'

Her mind seemed quite unable to accept these suggestions, as though it was overfull and couldn't make space for them.

'You aren't looking at all well,' he had said. 'I think this has all been too much for you.'

'I don't feel able to plan ahead. I'll be all right if I just take things step by step.' She wasn't even sure of that.

He had been dismayed. Usually, if there was any planning to be done, she was the one who must do it. She couldn't summon the energy to reassure him; she felt old and dry as a squeezed lemon, all the zest wrung out of her.

The waitress hovered. Either she must order another coffee or vacate the table. She paid the bill and went out into the teeth of the wind. Memories of other unseasonably cold days came to mind. 'Stow-on-the-Wold,' she muttered to herself. 'I'm too old to face into the wind now.' She turned about.

181

At the end of the street there was a great mound and one tower of the castle peeped out from a dense mass of trees. It reminded her of a castle in France beneath which she had stood one blustery autumn day. How inexorably one is led. This morning when the French party arrived at the farm she had fled in panic like a fugitive. But driving across the moor she had had no sense of having escaped. 'Something treads on my heels,' she had thought, 'and day by day it gains on me.'

And so now, standing still on the pavement, an awkward obstacle round which people must make their way, some turning to stare resentfully, she saw the red ball bounce out of the crowd and stop, trapped at her feet. A boy of about seven came running after it. The face turned up to her was Teresa's — the likeness was beyond all questioning, although she had questioned it many times since that moment.

'It's all coming at me too fast now,' she said, standing there in the street, blocking the way, seeing the face of the child, a face full of mischief of the kind that only the confident child can enjoy, unafraid to take risks with the tolerance of adults.

'Comment tu t'appelles?'

'She's a foreigner, poor dear,' an elderly woman said to her companion as they edged off the kerb to pass her.

'D'où viens tu?'

'Where is it you want, love?' A big, motherly woman had decided to take her in charge and was speaking loudly on the assumption that all unfortunates are deaf. She spaced her words, 'Where   do   you   wish to   go?'

'The church.' It was the only place she could think of

that might offer space and a chance to be left alone.

The woman accompanied her down a little street, which ran like a slip road linking the main street to the church green. 'There you are, love; you'll be all right now, won't you?'

It was a big church and inside there were few visitors. Clarice sat in the south transept where there was, if anything, rather too much space for her comfort. She longed for a Quaker meeting house, combining that atmosphere of simplicity and sanity which she needed as never before. This was too majestic for her; physically and spiritually it dwarfed her. It also posed too many questions.

From somewhere up in a corner of that vast fan-vaulting Teresa's child looked down at her, like the Lincoln imp, like the joker that prances behind the solemn procession, mocking and posturing, a black reminder that nothing is sure, that there is no such thing as security.

Teresa's child had told her that his name was Guy and he had pointed across the field to where slate roofs rose above the trees. It would make sense that Teresa should be here. This was an area where Clarice knew she and her family had spent several holidays, and not far away was the convent where the eldest daughter had made her vows. Clarice knew she had only to ask the child, 'May I walk with you?' and the torment of uncertainty would at last be lifted from her, she would know what it was that she had helped to bring about and the consequences would grant her absolution. But she had not asked. She had watched the child run back into the crowd kicking the red ball before him and she had made no attempt to follow.

Teresa had made a new start in life here, she had told herself. What right have I to cast the shadow of the past over it? In the great church the question echoed hollow. No breath of congratulation rewarded the selfless renunciation, the sacrifice of the soul's tranquillity. What could I have offered her, what gift could I bring? Only the memory of evil. Somewhere up in that fan-vaulting mockery responded to this pious protestation: it was fear for yourself that held you back.

Over the years it was the mischief in the child's face that had haunted her. Was it the lovely naughtiness of boyhood or the legacy of the grandfather? The risk of knowing what she might have helped to perpetuate had been too great and she had settled for uncertainty.

I was offered a chance and I refused it, she said; I was afraid of what might be shown to me and I have been haunted ever since. This time there was no mockery, only a dry acceptance. The joker had played his part and seemed to have departed. She, too, got up and went out of the church.

Horses' hooves clattered on cobbles, echoing in the constricted area, and from out of the narrow archway came a horse ridden by a girl of some twelve years. Horse and rider seemed surprised by their surroundings. The animal snorted and tossed its head while the girl looked around fearfully, plainly a stranger to these noxious alleyways. She was dressed in a velvet cloak with a hint of fine silk beneath; castle rather than cottage was her natural setting.

'Help me,' she said to Joan, presenting herself with the

confidence of one who has no need to fear that her commands will not be obeyed.

'Aye, that I will, if you'll but tell me how.'

The response to this reasonable request occasioned some uncertainty. Help did not usually require explanation. The girl considered her situation and eventually announced, 'I must be away from this place.'

Joan pointed, 'The market lies yonder, past the stables.'

The girl thumped the whip against her thigh in impatience. 'I don't want the market, dolt. I mean to be away from the town.'

The words hung in the air, detached from the speaker, who seemed aware for the first time of their import. She sat staring ahead, like a boy who having announced his intention of running away to sea finds himself surveying the vastness of the ocean. Her face crumpled in the helpless grief of childhood forever confronted by matter beyond its control.

She said, 'They mean me to marry Sir Andrew Pellow and he is old and ugly and stinks abominably.'

She herself was rosy, dimpled and sweet smelling. She looked at Joan, unbelieving of such a fate; a plumped pullet awakening to the nature of the feast for which it has been prepared.

Joan thought: this is my daughter. She had seen her son many times, but this was her first encounter with her daughter. It did not surprise her that the child should have aged so little over the years; she was vague about the ages of her children and usually imagined them as she had last seen them, give or take a few years. Her attitude to herself was not much different. When she looked at the girl, she saw herself in the bright face that seemed made for all the shining things which bedazzle a child's eye.

She said, 'You shan't marry him if you don't want to.'

The girl dismounted and came to sit beside Joan on the broken wall. She seemed not to think it odd to talk to this old bundle. 'You are with the travelling players that have recently come to the town,' she said. 'My maid told me there is a woman among them who knows the way of a person's life just by looking in their eyes as you look in mine now.'

Joan had never told anyone the way of their life by looking in their eyes, but she was prepared to try. What had she to give? Only her dreams, it seemed. They had never been realised, never put to use, and so must be in very good condition to hand on to someone else. As the juggler created magic with his hands, she could spread pictures out before this girl as they travelled the road that would lead eventually to a village idling in a long summer's heat, people drowsing in trouble-free peace. She could conjure up the droning sound of the place, the smell of dust and baked earth, the warm sweetness of trodden meadow flowers, the sun closing sleepy eyelids. And somewhere a man such as the steward, proud as a peacock, with a strong young body and blue-black hair.

The girl thought she would like this.

'Then come with me, but you must leave your horse.'

'Then how will I get there?'

'You must walk.'

The girl considered this, weighing the inconvenience against the unpleasantness of Sir Andrew Pellow. She consented to walk, but with a look in her eyes that

186

suggested she would expect some improvement in her situation to follow quite rapidly.

Even without the horse, she would draw attention in any crowd. The juggler was good at creating fine fabrics; Joan wasn't sure he would be much help in making them invisible. She led the girl away from the market, impelled only by the certainty that these narrow streets could not stretch much further. The town was not large; one's eye encompassed it readily from the brow of the hill as one travelled towards it. Her instinct, always a better friend than reason, was right and soon they came out on the bank of a stream and saw the great church not far away, men pushing barrows and others loading buckets to be hauled up to the masons at work on a part of the roof. When she had left the juggler to find food the cart had been standing so that one looked across the spine of the church to the tower. She urged the girl forward, 'This way, this way. We must cross the stream into the field.'

There were many travelling people in the field now and the townspeople were beginning to drift over from the market. The juggler was distinguishable for his lack of activity, sitting hunched with his head in his hands and Joan knew that he feared he had lost her. It would not have occurred to him to have left the cart unguarded to find her; he fretted about each spoke in each wheel in case the cart should come to harm and leave them stranded. When he saw her he jumped up and struck her for putting him in such despair. They fell to quarrelling and fighting, which was rare for them, and by the time they had finished the mutton tarts she had saved for him were mostly spoilt. They had also attracted attention.

At the far side of the field a small body of armed men was making its way through the crowd, pausing every now and again to push open booths or look inside tents, clubbing to the ground any who impeded their progress. Nearby, people turned to look at the girl, standing in the shelter of the cart, holding her cloak around her and trying to look disdainful, though fear darkened her eyes.

'Leave her,' the juggler said to Joan.

'But she is . . .'

'She is nothing to us, leave her. We must get away from here.' He tried to drag Joan into the cart.

But she was not going to run away; she had run away once before and it had been a sore trouble to her ever since, so this time she would stand her ground even if the whole town burnt down around her.

'She is my daughter,' she cried as the armed men advanced through the crowd. 'She is dressed in these fine clothes for a pageant . . .'

People began to back away from her. She and the juggler had a small patch of ground all to themselves – which was nothing new, it happened whenever they entertained at a fair. She clapped her hands and cried to him, 'Show them. Show that they've made a mistake, that she is our child and we will act for them . . .'

But his face was white and his eyes were wide with horror, just as they had been that first time when he came in from the dark and found the Duke of Clarence's man lying dead in the kitchen. 'Act it for them,' she cried. 'They're so stupid, they don't understand words; but you can make them see it. She is our daughter and we are here to perform for the townspeople.'

The men with weapons were thrusting their way towards them. A babble of voices broke out. 'It was her, she brought the lass here. She dragged her here, we saw it.' They began to throw stones as proof of their virtuous intent.

The juggler cried, 'She is ill. She doesn't know what she says or does.' His voice was weak, he had no gift for words; but he was agile and he danced in front of Joan, warding off the stones the people were throwing. 'Please, she means no harm. Let me take her away.' He capered in front of the first armed man to emerge from the crowd. 'I'll take her away, she won't do any more harm. I'll beat her once we get away.'

The man swung the butt of his weapon and said, 'You'll not be beating anyone.' The juggler dodged that blow, but the next caught him on the shoulder; even so, he was nimble enough to avoid another blow aimed at his head. But there were too many men by now and he had always needed space for his graceful art. They bore him down. The crowd clapped and cheered and several people ran forward to hold the girl in case she should get away and bring trouble to them all, but she was eager enough to be captured now, horrified at the ending of a morning's impetuous folly.

The armed men bore away their captives. They had left Joan and taken the juggler; he would be a more fitting malefactor to bring to the justice of their lord than an old madwoman.

Joan struggled while sweaty hands tore her bodice and nails scored her breasts; she bit and scratched, fighting for her child as she had never fought before. They would have to tear her to pieces before she stopped fighting. And so they would have done had not the people in another part of the ground, who had no knowledge of what was going on, suddenly surged forward in a great hurry to reach the castle gate where they thought, mistakenly, that free ale was about to be dispensed in celebration of his lordship's feast day. Joan fell to the ground and managed to roll under the cart while the thudding feet passed.

She was sorely bruised and for a time could scarce draw breath. When at last she raised herself on one elbow the crowd had gone and she was alone, save for an old tinker who was loading up his horse. 'They took 'm away, tha' fellow,' he said. 'Tha'll not see 'm agin. I saved this for 'ee.' He handed her a velvet cap which she had given to the juggler, having come upon it none too honestly at one of the fairs.

She sat holding it for a time. Violence had brought this quiet man into her life and violence had carried him out of it. She pressed the cap against her cheek, remembering the rich brocades and silks which he could bring before her eyes, the dazzling glory he could momentarily conjure from the simple trappings of life. In the days to come she would feel his loss more keenly than she had felt the loss of Martin. He was a good man and good men were hard to come by.

Later, as the sun dipped over the field, she dragged herself down to the stream to wash. Her face was mirrored in its still water and she saw that she was old, and as she looked, learning the reality of herself, she understood that her wanderings were over. The sun-baked villages where she would once again find the steward with blue-black hair no longer beckoned. For the first time in her life she knew where she must go.

'Here,' she said to the old tinker, seeing with what eagerness he eyed the velvet cap. 'I'll have no use for this now.'

She put her few belongings in two bundles and tied them to the long pole the juggler had used.

And Clarice, returning to the car park, saw her as she set out on her last journey. Their eyes met and Clarice said, 'Oh, my fellow wayfarer, how I wish we might speak to each other. Such tales we would have to tell.'

That night, walking in the starlight from the theatre, she paused to look up to the hills and saw, directly above her, a solitary figure silhouetted on the skyline. 'She has arrived at last,' she thought.

Nineteen

===

'THERE'S ANOTHER woman here,' Joan Mosteyn said to Dame Priscilla. 'Another like me. Only she wears breeches and her hair's been shorn, poor creature. What do they mean to do to her?'

'There is no such person,' Dame Priscilla answered wearily.

'But I saw her, and she knows me; she calls me her fellow wayfarer.'

Dame Priscilla did not see fit to pass on this latest instance of madness. In truth, she was very sorry to hear it, for Joan Mosteyn had seemed to be improving. She worked harder than she had ever worked since she first came to Foxlow Priory, bending her strong, vigorous body to whatever task was allotted to her.

Joan was taking note of the here and now of life. In the past there had always been something else that she was yearning to do somewhere else and mind and body had scarcely ever been in harmony.

She said to Dame Priscilla as she did the washing in the stream, 'When I was in my mother's house I slept in a little room with a window so high I had to stand on a bench to look out; all I saw was the tips of trees and stars. My mother said I shouldn't look out, that if I did I'd get carried off by Will o' the wisp. But I married Martin

Mosteyn. After Martin died and the villagers drove me out, I spent plenty of nights under the trees and stars, but Will o' the wisp never came for me. Even when I took up with the juggler and we went from place to place and all we owned was the horse and cart and what we could carry in our packs, even then I never did catch up with him.'

Dame Priscilla, recalling what the prioress had said about Joan gathering the threads of her life together, prompted gently, 'And then you came here.'

Joan said, 'Yes.' They both kept silence, Dame Priscilla thinking what a sad end it was, while Joan thought how wonderful it was.

Everything had been taken from her, home, husband, children, lovers. And now, at the end of it, he had gone, too; that vagabond Will o' the wisp whom she had followed for so long, beguiled by hope, had gone dancing off round the bend of the road and over the brow of the hill. She was stripped bare as a tree in winter. It was surprising how peaceful it was to be free of desire and expectation. In fact, now that she had nothing, she sometimes felt as though she had everything. It didn't stay with her, this contentment. She had her fits still when her body would go dancing and no one knew where her wits were; but the days of her peace outnumbered the days of her fits.

But for others there was no peace. There was sickness in the village and drought and the people were weak and starving. They looked back over past years, remembering disputes that had arisen over fishing and fowling, rumours about a nun who had conceived a creature up on the wild moorland, giving birth to a child with huge horns instead of ears, who had been buried alive at night. They remembered, too, that more recently the nuns had wilfully taken in a madwoman who had uttered dreadful curses and had undoubtedly brought misfortune on them all. Winter with its deprivations lay ahead; before it took its grip on them, while the blood was still hot in their veins, the men went out one night and raided the priory lands, setting fire to one of the barns.

The nuns watched horrified. The priory had been their shelter and was now their prison; perhaps it had always been prison to some of them, but they had not seen this so clearly before the flames came near. Dame Ursula was not the only one to see the devil dancing in the heart of the fire.

The madwoman became terribly agitated and it took three of the nuns to hold her down, else she would have rushed out into the flames. 'The devil calls his own,' old Dame Edith said grimly. They would gladly have consigned her to the flames had it not meant opening the gate, which was a risk they dared not take. Dame Priscilla went for the old priest. He was in his chamber, standing by the window watching the fire.

'We've held the cross over her and still she resists,' Dame Priscilla gasped.

'She needs chastising,' he said, without turning his head. This advice was hardly practical since Joan was too robust for the nuns to chastise even when she wasn't in one of her fits.

'One word from you, Father,' Dame Priscilla pleaded. 'One word and the devil will surely leave her.'

Joan had escaped from her captors and when the priest entered the kitchen she was pursuing the frightened nuns with a warming pan. The fire shed a crimson light on this violent scene and Dame Priscilla felt she had stepped into Hell. So, judging by his expression, did the priest. Joan came thundering down the side of the long trestle table, knocking over pots and pans and a bench, and the priest stood in her path, looking as though he had lost all power of speech and movement. Joan swung the warming pan above her head, holding it with both hands; and there she stopped, while the nuns held their breath, not daring even to pray, and outside the fire crackled and popped and the trapped cattle shrieked pitifully. For what seemed many seconds she remained poised, legs apart, as awesome as one of the forbidden gods the Danes brought with them long ago, the warming pan held aloft like the smith's mighty hammer, firelight burnishing her fearful face. Then she let the weapon fall behind her shoulder; one upthrust arm bent across her face to shield her eyes, the braced muscles of stomach and thigh relaxed and with a little sigh this magnificent creature sank languidly to her knees, where she became absorbed in an examination of her gown. She studied the coarse material, apparently in some perplexity as to how she came to be so attired. Her words when she finally spoke made little sense. 'And tell him to bring me a length of green say . . .'

She looked at them, standing around her. 'This is the time that the cattle are slain. Martinmas. Martin. And Piers and Jemima.' She gave a sharp cry and grasped at the hem of the priest's robe. 'What are they doing to my children?'

Dame Priscilla beseeched him, 'Tell her something good about the children, Father; it will give her and all of us some peace.'

'Your children live,' he said.

'They live,' she repeated.

'Yes.'

She seemed at a loss what to do with this assurance and sat back on her heels, looking uncertainly about the room. The fire was burning more fiercely than ever outside and all around the walls glowed rosily, which seemed to please her.

'Did the Lady send you to tell me this?' she asked.

There was such rapture in her face that none could doubt that it was not the priest whom she saw standing there. 'The Lady did send you. She sent you to tell me that my children are alive. Did she tell you where they are and what they are doing, and how they are, because I forget so much . . .'

The priest said, 'There is nothing else I can say. Sometimes, Joan, we have to be content with very little.'

She bowed her head. 'I am content,' she said meekly.

The nuns marvelled at how the light from the fire could so transform this mad creature that she might at this moment have been taken for a gentlewoman.

Then, as if by a miracle, it began to rain. It rained more than any but the very old could recall. Streams overflowed and the water, rushing from the moor, cascaded down, sweeping away whole farms and hamlets. For a time those who had surrounded the priory withdrew to shift for themselves and their families.

There remained an unpleasant stench of burning that try as they might they could not get rid of; it seemed to have become part of the fabric of the building and it was in their nostrils day and night. There were those among the nuns who had sometimes enjoyed dreams of being carried away and used vilely; the stench invaded even this pleasure and turned it sour. Prayer was no help; indeed, it seemed that they were most in danger when they prayed. As they contemplated the Blessed Virgin, there crept into their minds things that had walked the land before the days when the first saints came to bring the good news of Christ, dark things that had been banished to the swamps and the heart of the forest. These things were returning to claim back their domain. The prioress did not share these fears but she understood them, and at night she walked from window to window, from door to door, holding up the crucifix so that the things should know they could not enter.

When the great storm had passed, the villagers were in a worse plight than before. Joan Mosteyn pitied them. As she worked in the kitchen, helping Dame Marian, she said, 'Let me go to them. I will take them soup and nurse those who are sick. I was ever a good nurse. It is all I have ever been good at.'

As she spoke, she bent her head over the tureen, thrusting back her hair with one hand. Her hair had lost its lustre, but it was still thick and streaked with gold and it crackled as she ran her fingers through it so that sparks shot out around her head. Dame Marian started back. The soup had not smelt very wholesome for several days but surely this stench was more than humanly foul? Her flesh crawled; the old superstitions she had thought long conquered cried out within her, 'She is a witch.'

'We must thrust her out from here,' she said when she recounted this incident later to Dame Edith and Dame Ursula. 'Then we will all be safe.'

The prioress herself was confused.

'O Lord, what would you have us do?' she prayed. 'Were we all to be pure in heart as was your servant, King Henry, it would go ill with this your Priory of Foxlow, and even worse with the realm of England.

'Lord, when a godly king reigns, his subjects grow daily more wayward and undisciplined. What would you have us do? Were I to abandon myself to meditation forsaking the ways of the world, the world would cheat us of our lands and our dowries and we should not be able to carry on your work. What would you have us do?

'It was easier in olden times, the people had greater reverence, they made such generous gifts to the church that nuns and monks had themselves no need to store wealth and could afford to live humbly. That was a time when your saints could walk the earth. It is not so today. What would you have us do?

'If we send this woman out again to minister to the sick, they will think we have handed her over to them to deal with as a witch. If we keep her here, there will be no peace for us and worse than the harm to our bodies will be the corruption of souls. Many of the sisters are frail in mind and spirit, she is a threat to their salvation. Lord, what would you have us do?'

Twenty

THE FARM folk had the scent of the storm before it broke. 'Bad rain to come,' they said. The air was dank with it already. Eleanor reported that she had heard there were terrible high tides along the coast. 'Them'll drive the rivers back like they did in the great flood,' Harold said. No one knew exactly when the great flood had been, only that it was before living memory. Veronica had been allowed to stay a few days with another cousin who lived in the small market town some six miles away and Edward decided that she must be fetched back.

'The lass'll be safer there than here,' Eleanor said, but Edward was adamant that on no account should the family be separated at such a time and he set out soon after breakfast.

Rhoda had told herself that if she could but hold out for one day she would be on the way to mastering her feeling for Jory. But now a new and terrible urgency presented itself. As she listened to the talk of the coming storm, presented in the graphic detail that delighted Eleanor, and reinforced by the usually more sober statements of Harold, she, too, surrendered to the expectation of apocalyptic disaster. It was no longer a question of holding out for one day, but of this one day being her only hope of ever seeing Jory again.

Had she planned her going, worked out details in bed at night, risen prepared to dissemble and manipulate, it might have come to naught, for she was no schemer. As it was, the resolution coming suddenly with no time for second thoughts, she simply walked out unobserved. Boldness, as so often, paid.

What she had in mind she could not have said, as she turned her face into the wind. Decision lay behind her. As far as she was concerned, the chaos Eleanor and Harold had predicted had already happened; her world had shifted and changed overnight. How it would eventually assemble itself was unimaginable.

Soon the path veered to the east, giving more shelter from the wind, which she no longer met head on. She was able to walk faster. Even so, in this weather, it would take her over an hour and a half to reach the parsonage at West Bentham.

On the side of the hill, she saw sunlight on the trunk of a single twisted tree, green and flickering as if underwater. Ahead, there was no sun and the folds of the hills were gradually losing their sharp outline. On all sides she seemed to hear water running as though the hill were a honeycomb of hidden streams.

Around her now there was no sign of animal life and very little vegetation, the grass thin as if growing on the crust of a great crater. 'The moor is cruel': she recalled these words from her childhood. Over the years, looking back on a place left behind, they had acquired an appeal, a suggestion of some grandeur missing from her life in London, a primitive strength. But Jory had said, 'We can't identify with land, make it into an image of ourselves. We are not hewn of this rock.' The path on which she walked was strewn with stones; she would be better walking on turf, but on either side there were boulders among which it would be only too easy to twist an ankle.

She was climbing towards one of the great barrows now, and the light was so poor that its girdle of heather and bracken was indistinguishable from the nearer pockets of bog that lay between tussocks of coarse grass. Water gleamed on the path. There was always moisture here because not far beneath the surface there was an impermeable pan of iron that prevented rain from soaking into the ground. When there was too much water, the barrow simply shrugged it off its great shoulders, sending it cascading into the narrow valleys to join the swollen rivers.

She walked on and up, stronger than she had ever supposed herself to be. For a time, she thrilled to the knowledge that she could so pit herself against the elements. She forgot why she was there, where she was going, there was only the intense excitement of the present. She felt fully alive to each moment and when her limbs began to shake, she urged herself on, passionate for more testing as the dark ferocity of the great hill loomed above her. The path was veering again, bringing her into the wind so that she must fight for breath. She turned her head to one side for relief and, straying off the path, she eventually fell against one of the standing stones. It was a heavy fall and she lay staring upwards, her face as blanched as the sky.

It was easier to breathe lying there. She concentrated her mind on it. After a time, her mind told her she should get up. Gradually, with caution now, she drew her legs up and rolled over into a kneeling position and there she rested again, holding to the stone that was cold and unyielding. She could see the dark flank of the barrow. Beyond, the more distant hills were like daubs in a child's painting. The sky was now inky black with a silver tassel shredding from the west. She was probably more than half-way to West Bentham. But it was of Edward she was thinking as the first spot of rain fell on her eyelid and trickled down her cheek. The fall had shaken her body but had focused her mind, and her thoughts arranged themselves with stark simplicity. She and Jory had talked of the meaning of love: Edward was the one given to her to love; if she failed him, he would be destroyed and Veronica would be left to bear the burden. She struggled up in panic, calling out the child's name.

Her madness had passed, leaving her weak. Had it not been downhill most of the way, she would never have made the return journey. As it was, she fell many times. Now that the decision was made, she saw in her mind as she forced herself onward, not the anxious people at the farm, but Jory waiting at the parsonage. She cried for him in his bitter disappointment, but she did not turn back. Hewn of the rock he might not be, but he was strong. He would continue to walk the moors and the plans for his school would kindle his enthusiasm when his spirits were low. The full force of the rain came, blinding her to all else.

In one moment, she was drenched to the skin. Encompassed on all sides, she made her passage like a ghost condemned to walk through a never-ending wall.

Pebbles and stones travelled faster, rushing past her, bringing mounds of mud in their wake. The path had become a river bed; water scored channels in the grass on either side, so that the hill was like a maypole with great ribbons of water running down to the valley. She no longer had any idea of what was happening; the force of the rain drove her on long after she lost awareness of purpose. When she left the barrow behind and reached level ground it was no better. The moor bubbled like a cauldron. She slithered and fell and staggered up, but now her legs sank to her calves in mud and she gained only a few yards before she fell again. She called her child's name, but could not rise. She was by now nearer the farm than she realised and the wind carried the call to the ears of one of the hands who was fighting his way along the path where she lay, driving the few cattle he had managed to herd. But for him, she must have died on the moor.

The peasants were in a desperate plight and in their despair they turned once more against the priory, claiming that witches were harboured there. Had not the mad-woman been sent to them with food and medicine, had she not nursed some of the sick, yet she herself remained untouched by the sickness? Two men had forced their way through the gate only yesterday and had been repelled by Dame Katherine armed with a pitchfork and Dame Ursula with a bucket of live coals. There was only one solution and they all knew it. The prioress had scruples.

'These people will ill-use you if you go to them again,' she said to Joan. 'Do you understand what I am saying to you?'

'I would go to them. I was ever a good nurse.'

'I would like you to think about what I have said to you. For your own sake.'

Joan looked blank, surprised to discover that she no longer had an own sake, and stared around her as if it might have fallen off somewhere. Dimly, she thought she saw the woman with the shorn hair, looking at her with great pity. The light was slanting through the slit window to her left and she raised her eyes, expecting to see the Lady there. Her expression was such that the prioress involuntarily crossed herself. 'She sees Our Lady,' she whispered. 'It is true, then.' But Joan had looked beyond the vision to light unmediated.

'I would go to them,' she said. 'I was ever a good nurse.'

She seemed not to see properly and the nuns helped, some might have said propelled, her to the door.

'She is blind,' the prioress said. 'Blind and ignorant. Lord have mercy on her and on all of us.'

The nuns gazed at the prioress and she gazed at them. Dame Ursula said, 'It is true that she is better able to nurse than most, because even the foulest stench does not sicken her.' This she thought a cause for suspicion.

The prioress said severely, 'We are called on to love all our fellow creatures, even the foulest among them.'

One might as well scratch the surface of a stone for a sign of love, she thought, looking at their obdurate faces. But when had the seeds of love been sown at Foxlow Priory? Devotion, discipline, sobriety and a modicum of practical good sense were what she asked of her nuns. Love had not been required of them; love was left to the men and women who moved about in the sinful world.

The prioress looked at these wretched women who were the living proof of her own failure to love, and found comfort only in the kindly face of Dame Priscilla.

Joan Mosteyn did not return.

'It was her choice,' Dame Ursula said. 'We only sent her because she asked to go.'

The prioress called them all to prayer in the chapel and she kept them there all through the day and the night. This they endured without complaint and were careful to keep their heads bent so that if any glow should be reflected on the windows it might not disturb their meditation. Incense burned steadily obscuring the smell of tar-soaked faggots.

There was a great mountain with flaming tongues leaping from it and she was climbing on a path that went round and round towards the summit – and all this was within her mind; it was her mind and not her body that spiralled endlessly up through the flames. Occasionally she glimpsed faces in the flames; Edward and Veronica, they too were part of the inexorable motion, glimpsed like people in a crowd seen from a merry-go-round. They held out their hands and she tried to reach them, but they passed out of her sight as her mind spiralled upwards.

Her body could not stand this. Her flesh was on fire; her limbs ached as if there were weights attached to them, the pain bit into her bones; at every breath she took a red-hot poker was driven into her chest. But her mind spiralled relentlessly, insisting that she climb higher and higher and higher.

She was very high now, the corkscrew pressure was

tighter and everything she had ever known was dropping away from her as the flesh peeled from her bones. But as the faces watching the merry-go-round swung into sight again she found there was one thing she had with her still and she thrust it into the man's keeping. 'The school, Edward, you promised . . . ' Her hand brushed the child's cheek as she swung upwards again into the heart of the fire, where she heard another voice say quite calmly, 'Now is my time . . . ' as one might speak of the pain of labour.

'Thursday,' Alan said over the telephone. 'More than half-way through the run. I wonder if you'd mind if Jeannie joins us? She always gets depressed in the second half.'

And she is in the second half of life, widowed, lonely and wanting someone to care for, Clarice thought. You have an animal instinct for survival, Alan.

'I was wanting time on my own,' she said.

'I didn't mean that.'

'But I mean it.'

There was someone standing out of earshot, but waiting. She put the receiver down and ran quickly up to her room. Too quickly; thumps of protest on the wall of her chest.

She sat on the chair by the window, trying to restore inner calm, letting her eyes dwell on the green hill now freeing itself of mist. 'You are given time to grow into your harrowing.' Those had been her words spoken to Alan; the clue that had eluded her at the time. This is my harrowing, all that has come to me in this strange place is my harrowing. I could hardly tell Alan that. Only those two women who have kept me company would understand.

Her hands were icy cold and crossing them she ran her fingers up the sleeves of her pullover as far as the elbows. Thus straitjacketed, she considered her position.

Thursday. Thursday's child has far to go. She was a Thursday's child; but she had been and didn't feel there was anywhere left to go. In fact, had a strong sense of its all being behind her, of having in the last few days made a resumé of her life. In giving the past its airing she seemed to have exhausted its usefulness; even Robert had lost his power to disturb her. There remained one thing from which she had not yet been set free.

At least the blood was circulating well enough to have warmed her hands. She went into the bathroom, took a pill and examined herself in the mirror. A wan sight she made, face pallid and crumpled as old wash-leather. Whatever happened, she had an instinct to get out into the open, away from this house where the walls of her mind, let alone her chest, seemed to be breaking down. She put on an anorak and went out of the room and down the stairs, feeling rather like the lollard who must pass through a testing time before he sits down to his next meal.

Her little local difficulty was waiting for her in the porch, a tall young Frenchman who said, 'Excuse me, Madame – I see in the book of visitors the name Clarice Mitchell. And only you are staying here – so . . . ?'

'I'm Clarice Mitchell.' She felt as if a last account had been rendered as she admitted this.

'And were you . . . is it possible you were the head-mistress of Lady Catherine Prynne School?'

'I was.'

She was feeling in the pockets of her anorak, not looking at him directly. He said, rather grandly, 'I am Guy Matheos,' as if the announcement were normally accompanied by a roll of drums.

Clarice said, 'Oh yes?' looking suspiciously at the lining of a pocket.

'You would have known my mother as Teresa Davies.'

'I'm going for a walk.' Clarice was increasingly desperate to get into the open air. 'Perhaps you'd like to come with me.'

They went, by common consent, up to the moor. She kept her eyes steadfastly ahead, as if a close scrutiny of her companion might reveal some irregularity – that he cast no shadow, perhaps? For his part, he might have wanted a broad space for the enactment of his little drama, or it could have been that he realised he would not have her full attention while they were climbing. Or perhaps he merely waited for her to ask questions. For whatever reason, he said little at first.

They passed sheep sitting in the road, waiting for a passing car so that they could live dangerously. A silver-tan calf eyed them curiously from the shelter of its mother's flank. Further on, ponies cropped the thin grass and far below a river shone like a blue serpent weaving between the burnished swathes of bracken. Then the land levelled out into an abstract design in varying shades of brown, stretched to the horizon, its canvas scored here and there with tiny scratches.

Along one of these scratches, Clarice and the young Frenchman walked, and it was here that he said, 'I can hardly believe this. Two years ago I came to England and tried to find you – and now, quite by chance, we meet. It is very strange, is it not?' His voice, slightly teasing, suggested that what was really strange was the behaviour of this elderly woman, so inhibited she could not meet his eye.

'Why were you looking for me two years ago?'

'My mother asked me to find you. But no one at the school could tell me what had happened to you. And the telephone directory . . .' He mimed its weight in his arms. 'All those Mitchells! I was on a farming course and didn't have long.'

She knew that he was watching her face, sensing mystery and amused by it. As his grandfather had found life amusing? She said, 'Why did your mother ask you to find me?'

'She said she would like you to meet me. That was all. She seldom speaks of her life in England and we are curious about it. I expect she was a naughty girl? We know she ran away from school in England.'

But do you know she was thirteen at the time, Clarice wondered, and asked, 'Where did she go – immediately, I mean – that night she ran away?'

'To a farm where she had stayed *en vacances*. But the couple there are old now and very close; they tell little when we ask questions. You know the people in that region, they are close with everything. We have a joke that they don't like to give you the time of day. My mother went to a convent school not far away from there, where her sister is a nun. She, too, is very close.'

And how much could she say? Clarice wondered. No more, surely, than the close couple. He sensed a mystery and was intrigued, but there was no urgency underlying his curiosity. For him the reality of his mother's life was in France; probably he saw her as rooted in himself rather than he in her.

'I saw you once before, I think,' she said, because he expected her to say something.

'Surely not? I would have remembered.'

She did not pursue it because the more she told him the more she would have to explain and one thing would lead to another. She must be careful to give him no information he did not already possess. Somewhere out on the moor a curlew gave its bubbling call that sounded like a splutter of laughter and suddenly, as if he were looking over her shoulder, she saw the black joker that had gazed down at her from the fan-vaulting in Mellor church. 'Oh dear,' he seemed to say, 'so it's his possession of information we are concerned about, is it? His protection? Or are we perhaps afraid of the pit that might open up at our feet?' I haven't the energy, she protested; I have struggled against this for so long I have exhausted all my reserves.

In fact, she wasn't sure she had the energy to finish this walk; she could feel it running out of her so fast she almost expected to see it lying in a little heap on the path when she turned her head. Gower's words, that Alan would speak again tonight, came to mock her: 'Now our sands are almost run. More a little and then dumb. This, my last boon, give me . . . ' Why not? Could it be she had been too Puritan, asked for too little?

'Are you tired?' He was politely disappointed. 'Should we go back now?'

She went on walking. 'Tell me about your family.' As she said this she realised she had laid down a burden she had carried for too long.

'There is my mother and my father, who is a farmer also, and we are four children, two boys and two girls. I am the eldest.'

She had strength enough for the one last question. 'And your mother – all is well with her? She is happy?'

'You can ask that?' He laughed and stretched out his arms in the exuberant arrogance of young manhood. 'I am her son!'

She looked at him then. Full in the face she saw him and read what was there to read. He was less like Teresa than he had been when she glimpsed him as a child, the forehead broader, the nose straighter; but he had the same brilliant, deep-set eyes. What she saw in those eyes was that pure energy and zest for life that must have been his grandfather's when he was young and expectant, before the canker of failure had corrupted him. At the sight of that candid, unshadowed face, she experienced such joy that all her breath rushed out in a great cry of thanksgiving.

He was kneeling beside her, folding up his anorak to put under her head. 'I'm all right,' she gasped, wondering why he should be so concerned.

It grew very hot, there must be a fire in the heather. She could not breathe, the heat scorched her throat, seared her lungs. For a time she lost all thought in the struggle for breath. And then she saw them standing around her, the still forms with the archaic faces; like pillars of fire they stood. Now is my time, she thought, and closing the book on her lap she got up and walked between them into darkness where it was neither hot nor cold.

There was a moon and she walked along the path that led to the farm. She was alone and nothing stirred. In the distance there was a dark building with a single light silhouetted against the night sky and when she came closer she saw that the light shone above the sign of a wayside inn. The door was open and a tall woman and a girl with a mass of tangled hair stood on the threshold, hand in hand, their faces grave and loving as they waited for her to join them.